MW01127030

Table of Contents

Dedication

To my husband Chris, my forever Valentine.

Acknowledgements

I am enormously indebted to many wonderful people who have helped in my journey to publication of Blissful Valentine.

Chris Gale, my husband and one and only valentine, who inspires and supports me in everything I do.

Carol Riccetti, my mother, who truly believes I can do anything.

Sara Benedict, my PA, web designer, formatter, inspirational coach, all-around-problem-solver, and friend. Blissful Valentine would have never happened without you.

Olivia Howe from Beautiful Promotions and Beautifully Broken Book Blog, who not only created an amazing tour and release party for Blissful Valentine, but also constantly promotes me and my work, I truly believe you are my long lost little sister and I'm so lucky to have such a great friend, fan, fellow author, and promotional wizard with excellent taste in music.

Jessica Valliere, who helped polish my manuscript and offered great advice along with many comments that had me laughing like a hyena.

Cindy Davis, my proofreader/editor extraordinaire who taught me so much in the last few months. You make my work shine and always go the extra mile to help me.

Viola Estrella from Estrella Cover Art who created my beautiful cover.

Rachel, Sharon and Kelly a.k.a. 'Girls Book Club' who are a great group of friends that constantly support and encourage me.

Thank you all so much!

CHAPTER 1 — NEW BEGINNINGS

Abandon all hope, ye who enter here. I focus on the words written in Olde English script along the curving mahogany archway. Ah, the inscription on the Gates of Hell, how fitting. Looks like I'm entering Dante's second level, set aside for those overcome with lust. There's probably a huge frat house planted smack in the middle of the pit of fire, surrounded by raging flames. I heave a sigh, shaking my head. Why did I let myself get talked into this?

"Hey Brooke, are we going inside or standing on the porch all night?" My best friend Lexie tosses a long brown curl over her shoulder. "Come on, I'm freezing." She bounces on her toes, shivering.

Guess it's now or never. "Welcome to hell," I mutter, yanking the door open to shuffle forward into the foyer.

Lexie looks up at the letters. "Let's see how much hell we can raise at our first ever frat party." She nudges me, shutting the door to block out the frigid air.

The dingy green carpet in front of me meets tan walls showcasing posters of half-naked women holding beer. A plethora of bodies line the small space. How cliché. A squealing laugh rings out, pulling my attention into the crowd of bodies in the jam-packed room. A group of scantily-clad women, who clearly think it's eighty degrees instead of thirty-two, lean against the pool table in the middle of room. Their extremely short skirts and tight shirts leave nothing to the imagination. Guess I missed the memo about the beach theme.

The bass line of a Lady Gaga song echoes through my chest. I switch my focus to the crowd forming a makeshift dance floor. Bodies bump into each other, moving to the music blaring through the house.

I slide off my coat and shake the few snowflakes that have attached themselves to my long brown hair onto the foyer floor. Lexie grabs my coat, tossing it along with hers over the banister on the stairway next to two other coats.

Turning sideways, and sliding between the droves sweaty bodies, I follow Lexie through the crowded room, grazing a few with my elbows on my way. The crowd opens up and parts to one side of the room; most of them leaning against the chipped white countertops. A silver keg in a bucket full of ice sits at the edge of the room near the door leading to the back yard. Two guys in dark green Beta Omega T-shirts sit in lawn chairs on either side of the keg, sipping from red cups, nodding their heads to the music. A menagerie of pitchers filled with a variety of rainbow-colored beverages line the countertop. I trudge across the tattered linoleum to the center island and pull two red plastic cups from the stack.

I turn toward Lexie, handing her a cup. "Pick your poison." There's certainly enough of it around here.

"I'm sticking with beer." She heads toward the tap with a smile.

The guy sitting to the right of the keg jumps out of his chair as she approaches. He grabs her cup and fills it for her. She takes the cup and twirls her hair around her fingers with her free hand. The guy runs his hand along his buzz-cut hair and slides his hand in his pocket. I watch the mating dance between them, torn between awe and frustration. So much for sticking together for the night. We're here five minutes, and she's already caught someone's eye.

I walk away from the pair toward the far end of the kitchen. Beer is way too bitter, maybe something sweet with a kick. I peruse the colorful concoctions and choose the red pitcher that smells like berries. Perfect. I fill a cup and take a sip. The sweet liquid glides along my tongue on the way down.

The house is filled with hordes of people getting wrecked and flirting. It's just like the parties I used to go to after our football games in high school. Whether we were at someone's house whose parents were away, or partying it up in the woods, it didn't matter. Same scene same result, and never worth the aftermath. I sip my drink. Well, I came, saw, bought the T-shirt, frat parties are now a thing of my past.

"Brooke."

I whip my head around to turn toward Lexie and plow into a tall solidly-muscled body. My plastic cup crushes in between us, spilling red liquid all over the front of my white shirt dripping down my jeans to the floor.

"Whoa, sorry about that," he says, quickly turning to grab a towel from one of the nearby drawers. He frantically wipes it across the stain near my stomach.

I step back and look up at his slightly messy, dirty-blond hair. "I'll live," I stammer out, taking the towel from him. My stomach flutters as our skin makes contact. I take a deep breath and step back again, trying to create more distance between us. At this rate I'll probably end up hooking up with a frat boy. No thanks, hook-ups are off my bucket list. Time to switch to nonalcoholic drinks.

He rubs his hand along the back of his neck. "Wanna borrow one of my shirts?" His eyes travel from the stain to my face.

"Yeah, take it off," a voice drunkenly hollers from somewhere behind me.

I shake my head. "It's okay, plus I doubt we're the same size." Going up to his room is the last thing I should be doing tonight, even if it is only to borrow a T-shirt.

He wipes his hand down his jeans and holds it out to me. "I'm Dean."

I look down at his faded blue jeans, frayed at the knee and continue up to his dark green Beta Omega T-shirt, hugging the outline of his broad shoulders and sculpted pecs. I slide my fingers along his and shake. "Brooke."

Wetting his lips with his tongue, they upturn into a small smile. "Brooke, I've got to make this up to you."

I drop my hand and scrunch my eyebrows. "No worries."

He rubs his chin. "I'll start by letting you know that Hell Fire punch you're drinking is made with grain alcohol. Go easy on it."

I turn toward my crushed cup on the island. Maybe he did me a favor by spilling it.

I nod. "Thanks for the heads-up."

"Hey Dean, we need you to help us with the next keg," a voice yells through the crowd.

"I'll be right back. Don't leave," he says, placing his hand on my shoulder and gently squeezing before jogging through the doorway, into the crowd. My eyes follow the muscles in his back as they dance under his shirt with every step.

"What happened?" Lexie breaks my trance.

I pull down my shirt, exposing the stain. "Had an issue with a guy and a drink."

"Can't take you anywhere." She nudges my shoulder. "Let me guess. That guy you were talking to? He's cute, where'd he go?"

"Some frat emergency. You know how important a full keg is," I say, shrugging.

She nods and sips her beer. "Yep."

I sigh and grab a chip from the nearby bowl.

She puts her hand over mine, stopping me from grabbing another chip. "You wanna leave?"

"The deal was we're staying until two."

"If you want to go, no biggie. We'll have a few drinks in our apartment, maybe order a pizza."

No way am I ruining her fun, a promise is a promise.

"Nope, I'm staying."

The guy with the buzz-cut comes up behind Lexie and puts his hand around her waist. "Wanna dance?"

She turns toward him. "Sure." She puts her hand on my shoulder. "If you change your mind, I'll be in here dancing with Tom. Just say the word."

"Will do," I say, nodding. "Hi Tom."

"Hey," he says, giving me the typical guy "s'up" nod.

Watching as they disappear into the next room, I grab another cup and head over to the pitchers. Hmm, what's the lesser of the evils? I peruse the choices and stop at the last pitcher filled with blue liquid marked *Virgins*. Perfect, must be non-alcoholic. Filling a cup, I take a sip. Yum, blue raspberry.

I turn my head from side to side, and step on my tippy toes, scanning the sea of people for those clear blue eyes on that all-American boy face. He's nowhere to be found. Wait a minute. Why am I looking for him? Dean is the exact opposite of what I need. It's like this place sucked all the rationality out of my brain. Maybe I should just try and find an unoccupied corner and wait it out until two.

I push through the line of people waiting to fill their cups at the keg and head through the archway into a short thin hallway lined with people and ending at a white door.

Bathroom line.

I walk through another doorway into a room with a handful of people. Two burgundy leather couches line the light gray walls and a huge wooden coffee table sits in the middle of the room. Wall to wall bookshelves cover the far end of the room and pictures of fraternity brothers from past to the present line the wall on the right. This has to be the meeting/studying room. I set my cup on the coffee table and sink into the cool leather.

The couch shakes like a small earthquake. I hold onto the armrest for dear life and turn toward the person ruining my few minutes of peace. The smell of tequila and sweat fills the space between us. My stomach rolls. Last time it felt like this I had food poisoning. The scruffy guy now sitting next to me with half-opened eyes, runs a hand through his damp rat's-nest of dark brown hair. I scoot over toward the edge of the couch. Time to plan my escape.

He moves toward me and throws a sweaty arm around me. "Come on, let's get out of here," he slurs.

I swallow hard and push down the small amount of vomit that made its way up my esophagus. "I'm good."

He stands up in front of me and yanks at my arm. "Don't make me carry you."

I pull away, the force knocking him backward.

Is he really planning on kidnapping me? Yeah, like he could carry anything right now. I'll be impressed if he's able to walk down the hallway. Oh God, what if I'm wrong? It's like I'm in the middle of an anti-drinking film.

Dean jumps over the top of the couch in a *Dukes of Hazard* move and lands on the cushion next to me perfectly seated. It's like he practiced the move a million times. He slides his arm around my shoulder. "Sorry bud, she's with me."

I fight the urge to stand up and cheer from his flawlessly choreographed stunt. Soft fingertips graze the skin under my collar bone.

The man squints and tips his head. "She can be with you later," he slurs and pulls at my arm again.

I yank my hand backward breaking his loose grip. "I'm a one-man kinda woman." I shrug. "Sorry, there can be only one."

The man holds up his hands and backs away. He trips on the coffee table on his way out.

Dean wrinkles his forehead. "Where'd you come up with that line?"

I sip my drink. "A line from a cheesy 80's movie."

He slowly slides his hand off my shoulder. "No way, *Highlander?*"

I raise my cup.

He leans back and looks me up and down. "Yep, you're perfect. Marry me."

I set my cup back on the table. "Wow, a marriage proposal because I know a line from a movie where the character's main goal is to cut the other's head off... It screams romance." I smile.

"Hey, everyone ends up dead in *Romeo and Juliet* so decapitation in *Highlander* works too." He winks.

I chuckle. Guess he's got a point. *Romeo and Juliet* is a classic. If poisoning can be romantic then so can beheading. "Flowers and candy don't stand a chance next to decapitation."

He shakes his head. "I get it, all girls want is expensive jewelry, fancy dinners, and a white knight on a horse."

Yeah, like anyone actually gets that. I press my lips together and hold back a smile. "I'll take John Cusack holding up a radio and blasting a ballad outside my bedroom window."

He flashes a sexy half-grin. "Nice, a girl who knows her 80's flicks." He tips his chin toward me. "Theater major?"

I scrunch my eyebrows and move my head back. "Do I look like I want to be a star?"

He scans my body, from my black, high-heeled boots, to my fitted, white, now-stained, shirt. "Hell, yeah."

My skin scorches from his heavy gaze. "I'm a double major, business and marketing." I grab my cup and slug down the rest of my drink. "How about you? No. Wait. Let me guess. Undeclared until junior year and until then it's all about frat parties and bagging chicks." Oh my god, what the hell am I saying? Real cool, Brooke.

I cover my mouth with my hand and slowly lower my fingers down my chin, dropping my hand at my side. "I'm sorry, looks like I had a bitch hiccup. I'm blaming the drink."

"What are you drinking anyway?" He takes my cup and looks at the few droplets clinging to the side of the rim.

"Blue stuff from the pitcher, it's pretty good." I sink back in the couch and turn toward him. "I'll get us refills." He stands up and looks over his shoulder. "By the way, I'm a double major too, Civil Engineering and Business. We'll have to have a Monopoly battle sometime."

He disappears into the horde of people. I cover my face with my hands. Maybe I should just find Lexie and tell her I'm leaving. Frat boys aren't the sit around and chat type. In the end it's all about the conquests. Guys like him don't end up alone at parties like this.

I take a deep breath and exhale slowly. I've got to get out of here. I stand up and stumble toward the doorway. The armrest of the couch catches my fall. Jeez, looks like that drink went straight to my head. Guess my tolerance is way below what it used to be. I wobble toward the hallway. Note to self: *no more high-heeled boots when alcohol is involved.* My ankles shake. Looks like tonight is full of epic fails.

"Hey…Brooke," a voice calls from within the crowd.

I stop and pivot. The room spins for a brief second. I concentrate on the silhouette slowly coming into focus. The backlight glows around the outline of his body like a god walking toward me straight from the heavens. I blink repeatedly. Flawless skin leads to a chiseled jawline. I focus on the dark green shirt flaunting the outline of his muscular pecs and torso. Was his body carved from a block of marble? I suck in a deep breath, forcing myself back into reality.

"Where you going?"

I shrug. "I didn't think you'd be back."

He hands me another drink. "Can't get rid of me that easy."

I exhale slowly blowing my bangs around my forehead. "You only have one life, if you value it, go home."

His mouth falls open and his posture stiffens. He leans in and brushes his cheek against mine. The faint scent of beer mixed with his musky cologne invades my senses. My skin tingles as he brushes a stray strand of hair behind my ear. "I live here, so I am home." He chuckles and leans back. "Never met a girl who's a movie buff. You're full of surprises, Brooke."

I exhale slowly, trying to return my heart rate to an acceptable level.

A bead of sweat forms along my hairline. It's like it just became thirty degrees hotter in here in a matter of two minutes. I roll up my sleeves and run my hand along the moist skin on the back of my neck. "I think I need some air."

He scrunches his eyebrows and steps closer. "Are you okay?"

I nod and walk toward the door. My thin shirt clings to my skin. Great, white isn't the best color to wear when you're sweating. I maneuver around the kitchen island. Everything gets blurry. Dean places his hands on my hips and guides me toward the door.

An arm entwines in mine. "Where you off to?" Lexie's eyes search my face. "Everything okay?"

I wipe my hand across my forehead. "Yeah, just heading out for some air. Meet you down here at two?"

She twirls her hair around her finger. "Call my cell if you want to leave early."

"Will do." I flash a quick smile and continue forward, desperate for fresh air. My stomach hardens. *Please don't let me hurl all over Dean.* Not the kind of impression I'm going for tonight.

Dean pulls open the door. I rush outside like a horde of zombies are on my tail. The crisp, cool, winter air blankets my skin, quickly extinguishing the fire flowing through my body. I stomp forward, crunching the frozen snow along the edge of the porch. I sit on the concrete step and set my drink beside me. My clammy skin meets with the few snow flurries, floating through the air. Goose bumps erupt on my bare forearms.

Dean wraps his arms around me. "Have enough of the frozen tundra yet?"

I run my fingertips along his forearms, lightly touching his skin in a pattern of waves. Why can't I keep my hands off him? I slither down, interlocking our fingers. Pulling his arms closer, I shift until they surround me. Musky cologne fills the air. I loosen my grip and nuzzle his shoulder. This frat boy just became my forbidden fruit. How can I resist him? I slide my hands at a snail's pace along the peaks and valleys of his muscular torso. His breath comes quickly the longer I trace the planes of his chest. Small puffs of white vapor escape into the frigid air. I run my hands up to his neck and pull him into an embrace. Ah, hugging him forever would be divine. I squeeze tighter. My heart mimics a galloping racehorse.

I moisten my lips with my tongue but my mouth is full of sand. I glide a finger down Dean's chest and lean back to grab my cup from the porch. I need to keep his body against mine. I scoot closer to him and chug the blue concoction.

A grimace forms. "Yuck, where's the non-alcoholic stuff I was drinking before? This tastes like battery acid." I set the cup down and rub my hands across Dean's chest.

He holds my wrists, pulling my hands away from him. "What are you talking about?"

I sway and gaze at him through my half-opened eyelids. "The Hell Fire punch just about did me in so I switched to the virgin drink."

He loosens the grip on my hands. "Tell me you didn't drink from the pitcher that said virgins on it."

I trace my fingertips along his lips, down his chin, and slide my hand along his shoulder, scooting closer until no space exists between our bodies. "Guilty." I chuckle.

He slides a hand between us and pushes away. I blink, focusing on my surroundings. He takes my hands and pulls me up. "Come on, let's go." His teeth chatter.

I rise to my feet, wobbling. My knees buckle and I collapse onto the cool concrete, laughing like a hyena.

Dean bends down and slides his hand under my knees. He hoists me up in one swoop. My head bobs as he walks into the foyer and up the steps. I hold him tighter and look over his shoulder on my journey through the unauthorized portions of the frat house.

Dean walks through a door and sets me down on a bed. "Here, drink this." He hands me a bottle of water from the compact fridge near the wall and sits beside me.

I take a slug and let the bottle drop to the floor. My heart pounds, ready to rip out of my chest and fly around the room. Might as well get the full frat party experience. I push Dean down onto the bed. Let's see the rest of this hot body. I grip the hem of his shirt, sliding it up and over his muscles. That's what I call a washboard stomach. His eight-pack abs glisten against the dim light. I dance my fingers along the peaks and valleys, up to his torso. He takes my hand and holds my palm against his heart. What's he doing, I'm not even close to done with him yet. I struggle to break free but all the energy leaves my body in a matter of seconds. I blink. Everything darkens. Then again, my eyelids barely hold open. What's happening? Panic mode kicks in. I fight with everything I've got to open my eyes. Darkness surrounds me. Everything goes black.

CHAPTER 2 — THE NEXT DAY

My heartbeat pounds in my head, pulsating throughout the depths of my brain. I rub my eyes and sit up. Oh god, bad idea. Sitting up just makes it worse. My body orients itself. A wave of nausea flows through me. I cover my head with my hands. An army of giants all trying to squeeze my head at the same time can't feel this bad. Bright rays of sunlight shine through the window. I squint, slowly opening my eyes. Everything comes into focus.

Blood rushes through my veins, thrashing against my skull. My heart beats a million miles a minute. I slide my hands down from my head to my mouth. A dark green Beta Omega shirt outlining an array of muscles lies in the middle of a soft red and blue plaid comforter. The room suddenly closes in. *Please tell me I didn't break my cardinal rule and hook up with a frat boy.*

I take a deep breath and slowly exhale, dropping my hands. Ok, maybe I can sneak out of here unnoticed. I search for my best escape route. The light gray walls of the small room boast Yankees and rock posters. Plaid curtains hang above the small window, perfectly matching the comforter. Can't crawl out of there. Maybe I'm secretly stealthy. Guess we'll see.

Dean lays still on top of a heap of messy sheets. His faded jeans, frayed at the knee, hug every muscle. That dark green Beta Omega shirt couldn't fit him better if it was custom tailored. God, girls would kill for that perfect skin. Not a trace of any blemish or scar. His long eyelashes sway as his eyes move beneath his lids. Good, maybe he's a deep sleeper.

I toss my legs off the bed, trying to make my escape. A loud thump resonates. Dammit. I look down at the wooden floor and stare at the heel of my boot, which just made contact. Wait a minute; I'm fully dressed, shoes and all.

The dark blue cotton sheets tousle and the comforter moves. I freeze, keeping every muscle still, except for my eyes. I stare at the other side of the bed, willing Dean to stay asleep. No such luck. He stretches, his muscles dancing underneath his shirt. A slight moan escapes. Tingles encompass my body.

He turns toward me and props himself up on his elbow. "Hey. You making a run for it or did you fall out of bed?"

He runs a hand through his perfectly messy mop of light brown hair. Those clear blue eyes sparkle against the rays of sunlight illuminating his face. Not fair, no one should look this good rolling out of bed after an extreme night of drinking.

I fold my arms across my chest. "Running for the hills."

He grimaces. "Ouch."

I stand up and move my hands down to my hips. The change in position makes my head bang against my skull. "Could you blame me?" I drop my hands to my sides and wrinkle my forehead. "What the hell happened last night?"

He sits up and leans his back against the wooden headboard. "Maybe I should frisk you for weapons first." He flashes a smile and pats the mattress next to him.

I tilt my head and raise my eyebrows. *Do I even want to know what went down? Ignorance is bliss.* I hold up my hands. "Weapon free." I crawl back onto the bed, sitting down next to him.

His bright baby blues turn on me, intensely. "What I'm about to tell you might save your life." He raises his eyebrows and tilts his head. "The rules of a frat party."

Why's he so concerned about my safety? My eyes roll in their sockets. "Yeah, I'm done with frat parties."

"Understandable, but just in case." He holds up his pointer finger. "Rule number one, nothing is nonalcoholic....ever."

I lower my eyebrows. "Then why have a pitcher that says virgin?"

He bites at his lip. "It said virgins—big difference." He holds up his pointer and middle finger. "Rule number two, if something sounds cute and sweet, it's most definitely pure evil."

My chest tightens and my stomach hardens. "Like you?"

He smiles, his tongue darting out along his lips. He holds three fingers in the air. "Rule number three, if you wake up in a frat boy's bedroom he's required to take you to breakfast."

I swallow hard, trying to push down the putrid taste in my mouth. Breakfast is the worst idea I've ever heard. No sense in adding vomiting on a guy to my list of great accomplishments.

I run my hands through my hair and tuck the loose strands behind my ears. "Not sure I can keep breakfast down."

He hops off the bed and heads over to the small refrigerator, pulling out a bottle of water. "Rules are rules."

He hands the bottle of water to me and sits on the edge of the bed. "Trust me, hydration is the key."

I twist off the cap and take a sip. The cool liquid perks up my senses as it flows along my tongue. "I guess a cup of coffee won't kill me." Then it's back to my apartment and away from this evil place, and the temptations it holds.

My black high-heeled boots crunch against the patches of ice along the sidewalk on the two-block walk to May's Diner. A soft breeze blows through my slightly disheveled dark brown locks. I fold my arms around my chest, securing my coat close to my body. Only four more months and these streets lined with dirty snow will contain green leaves and a multitude of colorful flowers. Winter always seems to last forever.

Dean walks along the left of me, near the part of the sidewalk that lines the street. His rosy cheeks almost match the dull red of his coat. He slides his hands out of his pockets and grabs the silver handle of the door to May's Diner. *Guess gentlemen do exist.*

Flashing a quick smile, I walk up the two steps leading into the small diner. Dean follows suit, and walks across the black and white checkered tiles to a table by the window. I slide into the red vinyl booth and slide off my coat. Just as I pull one arm out of the sleeve, the pocket vibrates. Dammit. No one knows where I am. I yank my phone out and read the screen.

Where the hell are you?

Did you hook up with that hot guy? Text me.

It's two a.m. and you're not here ☹

So you did hook up with that guy ;)

If you don't text me back by noon I'm calling the cops!

Crap. Lexie's going to kill me. I bite at my lip and quickly type a response.

At breakfast, be home soon.

There, now she knows I'm alive. Part of this whole crazy night is her fault anyway. She's the one who insisted we need to head to a frat party to gain the whole college experience. Hate to be the one to tell her, but it's overrated. I slip the phone back into my pocket. Thank god the fresh air lessened the pounding of my head to a dull thump. Maybe a little food would do me some good and counteract whatever toxins were put in my body last night.

I narrow my eyes, then rub my forehead, sliding my hands down my cheek to my mouth. "What was in the blue concoction from last night? You know, the pitcher marked virgins."

Dean fidgets with his fingers. "A few things. Some rum, blue curacao, pineapple juice." He pulls at his lip. "Ecstasy."

My jaw drops. "What?" I clench my fists into tight balls. "I was drugged last night!" The barely legible words escape my clenched teeth.

Dean looks down at the table and then back up at me, picking at his fingernails. "It makes you want to constantly hug and cuddle, like a virgin before they give it up."

The thrashing heat beat in my ears makes my headache return full force. Is he for real?

He runs his hand through his hair. "The pitcher has an E on it so people should know about the ecstasy."

I wrap my coat around my body, desperately trying to poke my arm through its designated hole. "Guess I'm not up on my code. Thanks for the lesson."

He stands up and places his hand on my forearm. "Don't go. By the time I found you again, you'd already downed a glass of the punch. No going back. I would've warned you if I was there." He puts his hand on his chest and then raises it, like he's taking an oath in a courtroom. "God's honest truth."

I sit back down and move my coffee cup toward the end of the table for a refill. Great. Illegal drinking, drugs, waking up in a strange guy's bed—what the hell else can I add to the list of idiotic things I did last night? I gaze at his soft lips, slightly quivering. Dammit, no matter how badly I should want to punch him in the face I don't. Guess I'm lucky I didn't end up with some creep who did god knows what to me. "That was my first and last frat party. Let's get this breakfast over with so I can go on with my life."

He lets his head fall back against the vinyl booth and exhales loudly. "Hey, all you need is a wingman and you can still party without any of the downfalls." He sits up and raises his eyebrows.

"What can I get you two?" The waitress steps to the table and chimes in, tapping her pen against a small pad.

I let my coat slide off my arm onto the seat of the booth. "Coffee and toast."

Dean slides his cup toward the end of the table. "Coffee and the Hungry Man's Special."

The waitress heads into the kitchen and returns holding a coffeepot. She fills our cups and tosses some creamers and sugar packets on the table. "The rest will be right out."

I dump a packet of sugar and a creamer, into my coffee. I take a sip. Ah, the pounding of my head lessens to a dull thump. The aroma of fresh ground beans instantly perk me up. Wait a minute. I took a drug that makes people want to hug and cuddle. Sure, I woke up fully dressed, as did Dean, but what the hell happened?

Taking another bracing sip, I set my mug down on the table. "Is the wingman willing to share his secrets?"

He slurps his coffee and narrows his eyes. "Maybe."

I tap my fingers on my cup and look down at the table. "How did I end up in your room?"

He rubs the back of his neck. "The punch kicked in and you were extremely friendly, and hot."

I lower my eyebrows and shoot him a death glare.

"No, I mean hot. E makes you hot and thirsty. We went outside to cool off and that's when you heated things up." He winks.

I cover my mouth with my hand, and then slowly lower it to the table.

He sips his coffee and flashes a half smile. "No worries. I carried you up to my room and you passed out on my bed. Good thing you had a wingman."

My god, he's right. If I drank that punch and hadn't met Dean, this morning would be going way different. I guess I should thank him, or beat the crap out of him and his frat brothers for putting drugs in drinks where unsuspecting girls like me end up high on E.

I bite my lip. "Maybe having a wingman isn't terrible." Closest thing to a thank you I can give at this point.

"Not all frat boys are assholes... Most of us are, but not all of us." He winks.

The waitress comes over and sets two slices of perfectly browned toast in front of me and two heaping plates filled with pancakes, bacon, eggs, and home fries in front of Dean. "You kids need anything else?"

I shake my head.

"No thanks." Dean stabs a pancake with his fork and takes a bite.

I nibble on my toast, trying to ignore the stench of Dean's breakfast. My stomach churns. *Please let me keep this toast down.*

"You know, I could use a wingman myself." He shoves a piece of bacon in his mouth.

I drop the piece of toast back on my plate and tilt my head. "Sorry, my days of partying are over."

He slugs a sip of coffee. "I doubt that." He shovels a forkful of eggs in his mouth. "Seriously, I could use a heads-up on which chicks to stay away from on campus."

I take another bite of toast. "Lesson one: no one anywhere ever likes to be referred to as a chick."

"See, I need you." He winks.

A shiver sweeps through my body. I dart my tongue along my lips, catching a few toast crumbs. "Why do I feel like I'm in the middle of a teen movie?"

He chuckles. "Yeah, this would make a great script." He slugs more coffee. "Want to be each other's wingman?"

Every brain cell screams no but I can't seem to get the words out of my mouth. It's like my body is part of a raging civil war. *Really? Wingman?* Seems like a creepy way to try and get in my pants. Except for the fact that he could have gotten into them last night and didn't. My stomach flutters. Guess it would be a good way to keep his idiot frat brothers away from me. Ah, what the hell.

"Okay, deal." I hold my hand out to shake his.

His eyes widen. "Deal." He slides his hand into mine for a firm shake.

I squint from the sun reflecting off the thin coating of snow along the roadway and sidewalk. The crisp breeze blows a few stray strands of my hair around, tickling my frozen cheeks on the three block walk to my apartment. The sidewalks are empty, except for a few people hightailing it to their cars. Dean slides his hands in his pockets. I glance over at his ruddy cheeks.

"Cold today." I fold my arms over my chest and pull my coat tight against my body.

He takes a deep breath of winter air. "Nah, I'm used to playing in the early season when it's still freezing."

I scrunch my eyebrows and turn toward him. "Playing what, beer pong?" I chuckle.

He raises one eyebrow flashing a glassy stare. "Baseball."

Ah, that explains the Yankees poster. I shuffle forward, my teeth chattering. "A frat boy and a jock," I say, nudging him playfully with my shoulder.

He flashes a quick smile. "Sounds like a death sentence when you say it that way. Does my full baseball scholarship redeem me?"

My lips upturn into a smile and I nod my head slightly. "Impressive."

"Even more impressive than my vast knowledge of awesome movies?" he asks, scrunching his eyebrows, holding back a smile.

I chuckle. "Maybe a close second."

I rub my fingers against the sleeves of my jacket, trying to generate heat. Note to self: *always keep gloves in your pockets.* A small gust of frigid air blows against my face. My teeth chatter. It's like it dropped ten degrees in a few seconds. This walk seems like it's taking an eternity. I trudge forward, my black heels slip against the ice forming on the sidewalk.

Dean looks over at me. "I bet you're more of a beach girl."

I shiver and meet his gaze. "As long as the beach isn't in Antarctica."

"You're freezing."

Wow, maybe he should change his major to rocket science. Standing here in the middle of the sidewalk won't make me any warmer.

He takes a step closer and slides his hand over mine. My numb skin tingles, causing goose bumps to erupt along my skin. He takes my hands, one at a time, and warms them between his. My muscles relax and I take a step closer, erasing the distance between us. He opens his hands slightly and blows warm air across them.

My fingers throb from the warm air's contact with my freezing skin. I close my eyes and breathe deeply, taking in the scent of fresh falling snow with a slight fragrance of musky cologne.

Dean lowers our hands. His eyes lock with mine.

"Better get you home before you turn into a block of ice."

I nod slowly, mesmerized by his stare. I take a step back and pull my hands away. "I'm around the corner, second house on the right."

We walk side by side through the winter wonderland of dancing snow flurries and gray clouds. Even though my fingers are throbbing and my toes numb, I trudge slowly as if I'm in no hurry to get home or to leave Dean.

Dammit. This is the whole reason I avoid frat parties. Besides getting drugged and waking up in a guy's bed I hardly know like some whore, now I don't want him to leave. It's like I regressed two years overnight. Thought I was done with drunken parties and random hookups after I grabbed my diploma and practically ran off the stage at Mountain View High's graduation. No need to gain the reputation of desperate easy party girl again. Heat creeps across my face.

I stop at the bottom of the driveway and glance over my shoulder at the cozy little Cape Cod house. I turn back toward Dean. "This is me."

His eyes shift from the black pavement to the top of the roof, and then lock onto me. He shuffles his foot along the driveway, kicking a few loose pebbles underneath the light coating of snow.

"Nice place." He bites at his lip. "Rule number four: Always walk a beautiful woman to her door." He holds out his hand.

I giggle and slide my hand into his, trying to suppress the smile frozen onto my face. I tilt my head and lower my eyebrows. "And where do these rules come from?"

He cracks a half-smile. "Secrets of the Brotherhood." He winks.

We proceed up the driveway, hand in hand, leaving a trail of footprints in the snow. My heels stomp against the concrete steps, knocking off the excess snow. We walk to the edge of my door adorned with the winter wreath Lexie and I made last week.

He turns toward me and rubs his thumb along my fingers. My body trembles despite a wave of heat passing through it. I take a deep breath, trying to control my pounding heart. He lifts my hand up to his mouth and places a soft kiss above my knuckles.

"See you on campus, wingman." He drops my hand and takes a step back. "We're gonna turn this town upside down." He waggles his eyebrows and hops down the steps.

I let out the deep breath I didn't even know I was holding, and lean against the railing. My weak knees are barely able to hold me up.

Dean looks back over his shoulder and nods his head right before he turns the corner. I dig in my pocket for my keys, jingling them until I untangle the house key from the rest. I slide the key into the lock and step inside, quietly pushing the door shut. I close my eyes and lean my back against the door, an ear to ear smile plastered on my face. My heart flutters.

"Whoa, must've been some breakfast," Lexie says with rolling eyes, digging her spoon in a bowl of cereal and shoveling a huge bite into her mouth.

I shake my head and compose myself. *Guess she wants to know what went down last night.* My muscles relax and all the energy surging through my body dissipates.

She points her spoon at me as she crunches a mouthful of cereal. "I want details."

I toss my keys on the counter and slide off my boots. "I promise, lots of gory details. But first I need a shower."

"Hmm, gore and you need a shower. Can't wait to hear this." Lexie chuckles, sipping her juice.

I shuffle through the kitchen and head to the bathroom. Like any shower can invigorate me more that Dean just did. I turn on the water and breathe in the steam. I close my eyes and step into the shower, reliving the highlight of last night in a few seconds. So, I guess I've found myself a wingman that I didn't even now I wanted. Or did I sign up for something more?

CHAPTER 3 – TUTOR

My eyes peruse the thick red letters stained on the top of the page like blood left over from a slaughter. I lower my head and sigh. Dammit, a 72. First physics test of the semester and I'm already a C student. I've got to nip this in the bud before it threatens my scholarship. I pop a mint in my mouth, trying to suppress the sudden onset of nausea overcoming my body. Dr. Jenners starts his lecture, reiterating the importance of the laws of movement.

I nibble at my fingernails and wait for everyone in the class to gather their belongings and head out of the mammoth room. Dr. Jenners leafs through a folder as the chaos calms to chatter. At least he's easy on the eyes. Dark brown hair tinged with a few lighter strands, and an athletic body. Not what you'd expect a physics professor to look like. If his willingness to help students is as good as his looks I might have a shot of passing this class.

I shove my folders and notebooks into my backpack and slide out of my seat. Clutching the strap of my pink backpack with clammy hands, I approach him.

He looks up from his folder and tosses it on his desk. "What can I do for you?" He folds his arms across his chest, accentuating an array of muscles.

A bead of sweat forms along my hairline. "I had a little trouble with my first test. I've got this scholarship and I need a 3.5 GPA to keep it. Is there any way I can bring my grade up? Maybe extra credit or something?"

He nods and rummages through some sheets of paper scattered across his desk. "There's a tutoring program sponsored by the student union. Some of my top students from last semester are involved. I recommend you take advantage of the service, it's free."

I glance over the paper down to the physics section. Tuesday night in the Smithfield Hall from six to nine p.m. Perfect. "Thank you, I'll be there."

He smiles. "Don't sweat it yet. There's still time to bring up that grade. I think the tutoring will do the trick." He takes the manila folder he's been leafing through from his desk and peruses the papers.

I flash a quick smile and turn away, hopping up the steps to the exit. So I guess there's still hope. Maybe if I get to the tutoring session early enough I can pick the Stephen Hawking of the group to work his magic on me.

I glance at my watch. Almost time to meet Lexie for

lunch. I zip up my jacket, pull on my gloves, and push open the heavy door. A gust of frigid wind whips my hair along my cheeks and sends a multitude of snow flurries rushing into my face. I close my eyes, grip my backpack tight, and trudge forward as if I'm taking on a blizzard in the frozen tundra. The cold wind burns my cheeks. Just a few more feet and I'm at the dining hall.

I open my eyes for a split second but it's too late. A wall of pure muscle slams into me like a ton of bricks. I fall backwards, my hands flailing in the air for a few seconds before my butt smacks into the hard concrete sidewalk. My backpack flies into a mound of snow and slowly slides down the icy surface to the frozen ground. I blink a few times and try and focus on the face hovering above me.

"You okay?" Dean holds out his hand.

You've got to be kidding me. Heat spreads across my face like wildfire. First the physics test, now this. Do I dare ask what else is in store for me today? I prop myself to a sitting position and take his hand. He pulls me to my feet with one swoop.

"Come on, I can't let my wingman freeze." He grabs my backpack from the snowy mound and guides me forward, holding open the door to the dining hall.

I look up at him and lose myself for a minute in his

deep blue eyes. The chill miraculously leaves my body. Amazing, how could I have possibly not noticed him first semester? An elbow grazes me as a girl sprints toward the dining hall. I flinch and knock myself back into reality. Yeah, probably because I was studying all last semester, instead of allowing distractions to make me lose my focus. Maybe I should follow my own advice.

I fling my backpack over my shoulder and head into the dining hall. I sniffle and tuck a few damp strands of my hair behind my ear. "Sorry, blinded by snowflakes."

He pulls off his stocking cap and tousles his hair into a perfect mess. "Ah, happens to all the beach girls." He shakes a few snowflakes off his hat. "Lunch is on me. Least I can do after almost plowing you into a snow bank."

I bite my lip. "Let me guess. It's an unwritten rule that all fraternity brothers have to buy a girl lunch after they almost plow her into a snow bank?"

He chuckles. "No, but it should be." He takes a step forward and gestures for me to follow.

Crap, Lexie's waiting for me. I reach out and grab his arm. My hand barely gets around a quarter of his hard bicep. A surge of electricity flows through me. Holly hell, he gets more impressive by the second. "Can't today. Rain check?"

He nods. "It's a date." He winks and takes off down the hallway.

Wait. I never agreed to a date. My body heat rises a few more degrees, flushing my face. We're just friends. That's it. It can't go any further or it's destined to end up a disaster. Now, if I keep saying it to myself maybe I'll believe it too.

I drag a french fry through the mound of ketchup on my plate, forming a circular design. So I inadvertently made a lunch date with Dean. It's like my body is on autopilot, doing whatever the hell it wants despite my brain. I stare down at my edible art and try to clear my mind from all things related to Dean.

"So, I get it. He's supposed to protect you from sleazy guys and drinks spiked with god knows what at parties, but what are you supposed to do for him?" Lexie sips her diet cola. She twirls her hair around her finger.

I shrug and glance around the light gray walls of the dining hall. "I guess he wants me to give him intel about girls on campus…you know, who to stay away from and whatnot."

Lexie raises her eyebrows. "Does this mean we're hitting more frat parties?" A small smile creeps across her face.

I push my plate away and shake my head. "No, but if we do happen to make an appearance, I won't have to worry."

Lexie bounces in her seat. "Awesome. Remember that guy Tom...you know the one I was dancing with at the party?"

I tap my fingernails on the table. "Vaguely."

She takes a bite of her turkey sandwich and drops it back on the plate. "Well, he asked me to go for pizza tomorrow night." She wipes her mouth with a napkin and smiles. "Since he's in Beta Omega, frat parties may be back on the menu."

I sigh. Great, just what I'm hoping for. "The only thing on my menu right now is finding a physics tutor."

"If the rumors are true, wear a short skirt and heels and you'll ace the class."

I slug my water. "I don't know if pole dancing in the middle of his desk could help me now."

She stands up, grabs her backpack, and slings her purse around her shoulder. "Can't hurt." She nudges me as she walks past my chair. "Got English Lit in ten minutes. See you later."

I wave and sink back in the plastic chair. Hate to break it to her but frat parties are a thing of the past. Suppose we do go to a frat party and Lexie parties with Tom, and Dean acts as my wingman, and I give him the intel on the girls of the campus just as planned. Then what? Eventually, Dean will find one worthy enough to hook up with. So what's the plan for that scenario? Guess I'm supposed to sit outside the door and wait until he's done. How did I let myself get talked into this? Those deep blue eyes mesmerizing eyes are clearly weapons of mass destruction and I'm not willing to be a casualty.

I pull open the heavy wooden door of Smithfield Hall and wipe my wet boots along the black carpet. The intricate wooden carvings in the molding of the mahogany make it look more like a gingerbread house than a study hall. Well, except for the floor-to-ceiling bookshelves gracing three of the four walls. Five long tables, adorned with dark green lamps, spaced out almost equally, fill the room. I clutch the strap of my backpack and walk forward.

Looks like I'm the first one here. Great, am I the only

person who needs tutoring help in physics? Guess it would be nice if the tutors were actually here. I drop my backpack on the second to last table and slide into the hard wooden chair, arranging my tablet and physics book on the table along with two ink pens.

I take one from my meticulously arranged menagerie and tap it on the tabletop. Too bad patience isn't a virtue I've been blessed with. I pull out my cell phone from my backpack and check the time: six o'clock on the dot. Looks like the tutors aren't so punctual.

The door crashes against the doorjamb and slams shut, sending a loud thump through the quiet room. I jump and stare straight ahead. Heavy footsteps stomp toward me, louder with each step. I push my chair back and stand up, trying to get a better look at whomever is coming toward me.

I squint and try to focus as the figure steps into the dim light. It can't be. I rub my eyes and stare. Dean breaths heavy and throws his backpack on the table top next to me.

He pulls off his hat and runs his hand through his hair. "Ready to learn the laws of attraction?" He pulls out a chair and plops down, pulling it closer to mine.

My eyes travel along his chiseled jaw line to his cheeks, tinged with the slightest hint of red from the frozen air outside, and continue to his deep blue eyes. I lock my gaze with his. So far, the laws of attraction seem pretty unfair. I mean, my body refuses to acknowledge anything my brain is saying.

I sit back in my chair and turn toward him. "Are you stalking me, or are you secretly a superhero who feels the need to continually come to my aid?"

"Super Dean at your service." He pretends to rip open his shirt like Superman.

I roll my eyes and try to hold in the small smile creeping over my face. "No one else at Lakeview U needs physics help except me?" I look around the desolate room.

"Next to Organic Chem it's the busiest session." He pulls out a book and notebook from his backpack. "Dr. Jenners stopped me in the hall, told me he sent Brooke Powers to a session. Too bad he had an old flyer, Physics tutoring moved to Wednesday." He grabs an ink pen and slides it behind his ear. "What kind of wingman would I be if I left you hanging here all by yourself?"

"Your wingman duties are very diverse." I look down at my notes from yesterday's class.

He turns my chin toward him and crinkles his forehead. "Expecting someone else?"

A flash of heat travels from my head to the tips of my

toes from his touch. I breathe deep and look into his eyes. "Didn't know you were a science nerd too."

He drops his hand and turns the pages of his physics book to the laws of movement. "There's a lot you don't know about me." He raises an eyebrow.

"Ditto." I smirk and turn to a clean sheet of paper.

"Can't wait to be enlightened." He winks and pulls the physics book closer to us. "How does a business/marketing major end up in a physics class?"

I grimace. "Diversity credit requirement. Nothing else would fit in my schedule." I click open my ink pen. "How about you?"

He reaches behind his ear and slides his pen, letting the bottom edge brush against his cheek. It slides over his lips as he brings it down to the paper. "Lots of physics in Civil Engineering, plus it helps with my game."

I crinkle my forehead. "Really? Girls think physics is hot?"

He flashes a sexy half grin. "Baseball." He nibbles on the cap of his pen. "The force of the swing sends the ball in whichever direction the trajectory indicates. It's all about acceleration and velocity." He turns toward me. "Plus, some girls think it's sexy."

I roll my eyes. "Whatever. Here's the deal. I've got to

get a 3.5 to keep my scholarship. So far, I'm at a 72. Your mission, if you choose to accept it, is to help me get a 90% or above on my next test."

"I'm always up for a challenge." He leans in so close the faint scent of his musky cologne fills the space between us.

Tingles shoot through my body. Great, I was hoping for someone with a bow tie and glasses as thick as Coke bottles to tutor me. Whoever made the physical stereotype for a physicist clearly hasn't met Dr. Jenners or Dean.

"Let's make this interesting." Dean taps his pen against his lip slightly nibbling on the end.

My eyes follow the path of the plastic lid, sliding along the crease in his lip. "That would be a miracle."

"One of my job requirements." He raises his eyebrow. "If you get a 90 or higher on this test, we go out to celebrate."

"Sounds like a bribe." I tip my chin and raise my eyes.

"A wager. Plus I can put my wingman abilities to use. Since you won't party at the frat house."

This whole wingman thing is getting ridiculous. All talk no action. Does he really need me to get him the dirt on the girls on campus or is this a ploy for something else? "How does this wingman thing work again? It seems kinda one-sided." I tap my fingernails on the table.

He lowers his eyebrows and flashes a half smile. "What's the scoop on Tanya Layton?"

Other than the fact that she hasn't spent a night in her dorm room alone since she enrolled at Lakeview U and the rumors that she's sleeping with Dr. Jenners are most likely true, not much. God, he's actually into the whole better-than-thou-cheerleader-can't-live-without-makeup kind of girls. Whatever.

I cross my arms and tap my foot on the hard oak floor. "She's dating an older guy."

"Really?" He taps his pen on his chin. "Guess she forgot about him at the end of the semester party before winter break. Thanks for the intel." He salutes me.

"Always trust your wingman." I smirk and gaze down at my notes. *Please tell me he didn't hook up with her.* I mean, he deserves better. Sure she's beautiful and flirty but she's just...not right for him. I leaf through a few pages of my notebook. "Time to get back to physics."

He pulls my test paper out from the cardboard cover of my tablet and scribbles on the top of the page. "You got this one wrong: Newton's third law: When one body exerts a force on a second body, the second body simultaneously exerts a force equal in magnitude and opposite in direction on the first body."

Hate to break it to him but Newton got these laws completely wrong. No matter how much I try to exert the opposite force, my body flips everything around and I'm drawn to Dean like two magnets with opposite charges. Guess that's where the whole opposites attract thing comes into play. Now, if I can only find a way to fight it.

Dean's sculpted bicep dance as he glides his pen down my test extracting wrong answers on his way. I shift my focus to his rock-hard pecs and continue to gaze at his chiseled jawline, leading to his soft pink lips sporting a natural pout. I've got no chance in hell of passing this test let alone getting a 90%.

I shake my head and jolt myself back into reality. "Yeah, it sounds like gibberish to me. No idea what he's trying to say."

He nods and bites his lip. "Let's try something."

Oh god, this could be dangerous. He moves forward and leans in, moving closer toward me. A jolt of adrenaline rushes through my veins and my heart pounds against my chest. I close my eyes and lean toward him. "What do you have in mind?"

He holds his arms out and presses his palms against my shoulder, nudging me backward. "For every action, there's action, an equal and opposite reaction."

I hold out my hands and push against his rock-hard chest. Maybe I actually have a chance of acing the next test if this is what studying entails.

He slides his hands down my arm to my wrist, lightly touching my fingers as he moves away. "There you have it, Newton's third law."

"Impressive." I catch my lip in my teeth and muffle a smile.

Hmm. Didn't expect quite so much hands-on work. Not that I'm complaining. I loosen my muscles and let my hands relax, grazing Dean's pecs as I pull my fingers away. My lips part and my heart flutters as my eyes take in the curves of his torso against his thin, long-sleeved T-shirt. I bet he does wonders for that baseball uniform. He's becoming more impressive with every passing second. Now, if I could just convince my brain that we're only friends and this is nothing more than a run of the mill tutoring session. Yeah, right. If I can convince myself that's true, I might as well take a shot at curing cancer.

I poke my head between the shoulders of the line of

people in front of me. Megan Teller flings her hair over her back, hitting me smack dab in the face. I flinch. Hope this isn't an indicator of how my day is destined to go. The crowd finally dissipates leaving a few stragglers in front of me, blocking my view.

I turn sideways and slither between a small grouping of bodies. Fingertips graze my cheek and grip my shoulder. What the hell is happening? I gasp and whip my head around.

"Grades are posted. What's the verdict?" Dean bites at his lip and nods toward the bulletin board.

"If someone didn't yank me away, we'd already know." I step forward and peruse the bulletin board, running my finger over the list categorized by the last four digits of our social security numbers. I stop at 0723, my last four digits, and move my finger across the paper to the grade. I open my eyes at a snail's pace and focus on the number before me. Oh my god, a 94%.

I jump back and turn toward Dean, covering my mouth with my hand. He raises his shoulders and holds out his hands.

I drop my hand to my side and flash an ear to ear grin. "94."

He lunges forward and picks me up, twirling me

around for a second, then slowly sets me back on my feet. I stare, lost in his mesmerizing gaze. He leans closer, his nose lightly sliding over mine. My heart rate rivals the gallop of a racehorse. His lips move closer to mine.

A loud thump echoes through the hallway pulling me out of the moment. I step back, creating some much needed distance between us. What just happened? I look down at my physics book lying on the dark tile opened up to the chapter on the laws of attraction.

I take a deep breath and try to return my heart rate to an acceptable level. Fidgeting with my fingers, I quickly take the book and slide it back in my back pack, zippering it tightly.

Dean runs his hand through his hair and slides on his black stocking cap. "Mission accomplished." He flings his black backpack over one shoulder. "Wildcats at eight?"

I run my finger along the base of my neck and reach down for my backpack. "Huh?"

"Remember, our wager. Time to knock back a few and celebrate."

I've got to stop getting myself into these arrangements. Hanging out at Wildcats is almost as bad as going to a frat party. Not going to happen, not even if I got a perfect score. I narrow my eyes and purse my lips.

"Not a fan of Wildcats. Plus, I'm the one who ace'd the test. Shouldn't I get to decide how I want to celebrate?"

He tips his chin. "Lady's choice."

"Pizza and a chick flick."

His face erupts into a full-out smile. "Dinner and a movie. You got it." He takes a step back and turns toward the door.

My stomach hardens. Dammit. I just turned this friendly celebration into a flat-out date.

CHAPTER 4 — DATE?

I huff and throw my hands in the air. There's just no way to prepare for tonight. Nothing is right. Rummaging through my closet, I try to find the perfect outfit that says I care about what I look like but we're not hooking up. I guess the fashion gods have forsaken me. Such an outfit just doesn't exist. The hangers fly across the metal rod, emitting an ear-piercing shriek as I push through the multitude of shirts, tank tops, and sweaters. Well, going naked won't help my dilemma so I've got to pick the lesser of the evils.

My thin, red V-neck sweater and a pair of dark fitted jeans will have to do. I glance in the mirror and fluff my hair with my hands, readjusting the dark strands into place. Just two friends, who happen to be the opposite sex, seeing a movie and grabbing a pizza to celebrate the victorious reign over the physics test. My heart quickens.

A loud knock on the door echoes through my room, pulling me out of my thoughts. I jump into my jeans and hop to the door, sliding them up and zippering them on the way. I pull open the door and take a step back.

"Hey, you look hot for your non-date." Lexie nudges my shoulder and sits on my bed.

I plop down on the purple comforter next to her. "Couldn't find the perfect non-date outfit." I roll my eyes and shake my head.

She presses her lips together trying to hold back a smile. "You know it's a date, right?"

I hop up and fold my arms across my chest. "Can't a guy and a girl just hang?" My lips press into a white slash.

Lexie twirls hair around her finger. "What's the big deal anyway? He's cute, nice, and he's got a hot body… Let me guess, you're looking for an unattractive, mean slob?"

I grab a pillow from the bed and throw it at her, trying to muffle a giggle. "You know I don't date Beta Omega brothers. I've got to focus on school anyway."

She crinkles her forehead. "He's already your tutor. Seems like a win-win."

"I don't date frat guys," I say as I grab a pair of black boots out of my closet and slide them on.

"We'll see how long that rule stands." She winks and walks to the door. "I'm meeting Tom at Wildcat's. See you later… Oh, I won't wait up." She winks and closes the door behind her.

For someone who knows me better than anyone, you'd think she'd remember my will is as strong as steel. I glance in the mirror and glide pink shimmer lip-gloss along my lips. I smack them together and take a step back, adjusting my sweater so the deep V-neck doesn't turn this night from PG to R.

One thing's for sure, this whole wingman thing has got to stop. I mean, the whole idea of it breaks a million rules of girl code. And Tanya Layton, seriously? There's no way I'm getting to know her any better to give Dean the scoop. She's a carbon copy of the girls I used to hang out with in high school: gorgeous, easy, and completely dangerous to men. I know, I was one of them.

Dean's the furthest thing from her type anyway. She's all about the hot, rich guys, who buy her anything she wants and fall at her feet. It would be a disaster waiting to happen. Sure, Dean's got a smokin' body, probably from the baseball training. A memory of his chiseled torso floods my mind. Tingles rush through my body like an electric current. He's funny, smart, and cute in that all-American-boy kind of way. Every moment with him is a struggle. It takes skill to resist his charm. Not everyone is blessed with his charisma. He needs a girl who at least has a soul.

Maybe Lexie's right. Maybe Dean's not the evil frat demon I've concocted in my mind. Could he be the exception to the rule?

The doorbell rings, resonating through the apartment. I take one more quick glance in the mirror, fling my purse over my shoulder, and trot across the kitchen tiles. I pull open the heavy wooden door and gasp.

Dean holds out a bouquet of pink carnations. "Congrats gift."

I stick out my hand, trying to prevent it from shaking, and take the flowers. Holding them up to my nose, I inhale the sweet aroma. "You didn't have to get me a gift...but thanks, they're beautiful." I turn around pull a glass vase from the cabinet under the sink and set them in.

He runs his hand through is hair. "I've got a theme going."

"Theme? We're just grabbing pizza." I grab my keys from the counter, slide on my coat, and head out the door. Guess it's time to start this adventure.

I slide my hands in my pockets and walk down the steps next to Dean. A gentle gust of frigid air flows, causing a few loose strands of hair to tickle my face. "Okay, so what's the theme?" A cloud of white vapor escapes from my mouth as I speak.

"You've got to promise not to fall in love with me after I tell you." He turns toward me, flashing a sexy half smile.

I raise my eyebrows. "I think I can control myself."

He slides his arm around me and pulls me close. My heart thumps in an array of erratic beats. His rock hard body presses against me. Self-control, don't fail me now.

He leans in and whispers in my ear. "You wanted dinner and a movie, right?"

I nod. *Dear god, where the hell is he going with this?*

My feet shuffle against the remnants of ice-melt that sparkles against the sidewalk. We turn the corner and continue forward, about a block. He stops and twists my shoulders toward the large building on the left.

Leaning forward, he whispers in my ear. Soft lips lightly touch my lobe. "Retro night at the Commonwealth Theatre. I got us two tickets." He steps to the side and gestures with his hand. "Double feature."

My eyes peruse the letters lit up at the top of the sign.

Now Showing Pretty in Pink and Top Gun.

A smile creeps across my face. "Love the theme."

He holds out his arm. "Can I call ya Maverick?"

I slide my hand out of my pocket and interlock my arm with his. "Not if you expect me to answer."

"I never know what to expect with you." He steps forward and pulls open the heavy glass door.

Bet he won't expect this. I charge forward toward the snack bar as Dean hands our tickets to the usher. Hate to break it to him, but I'm not one of those girls that pretend they don't eat. I require more than alcohol.

He places the ticket stubs on the snack counter. "Let's get something that'll hold us over until we get to Gerardo's."

"Read my mind." I reach into my purse and pull out my wallet, setting it in front of me on the snack counter. "You got the movie, snacks are on me."

He puts his hand over mine and the wallet. "No way, it's a rule. You must treat the woman who slays the physics gods to a celebration of her choice."

A surge of tingles flows through my body when our skin makes contact. He slowly moves his hand away from mine, rubbing his thumb over mine. He gently pulls away. My heart stammers and my breathing becomes heavy. I hold up my wallet, trying to steady my trembling hand and drop it back into my purse. "Where is this list of rules?"

He holds up his hands. "Secrets of the Brotherhood. I

swore an oath."

I shake my head. An oath? Yeah, I vaguely remember the code of honor from my first, and last, frat party. I think it involved ecstasy, spilled drinks, and a ton of colored liquids.

"What can I get for you?" A tall, lanky teenage boy with thick glasses steps up to the cash register. Now this is how I imagined my physics tutor to look.

I glance at his nametag. "Hey Flynn. I'll have a large popcorn, large soda, chocolate covered peanuts, gummy bears, and M&M's."

Dean jerks his head back and lowers his eyebrows.

I shrug. "It's a double feature."

His lips upturn to a smile. "I'll have a large soda. Maybe she'll share with me."

Flynn looks me up and down. "I'd share with her anytime."

"She's one of a kind." Dean leans in closer and tucks a few stray strands of hair behind my ear. "Brooke Powers, you're the most amazing woman I've ever met."

My face flushes. "Dean…" I crinkle my forehead and tilt my head. "I don't even know your last name."

He smirks. "Hmm, you spent the night with me and don't even know my last name. Maybe you should join the fraternity."

Heat spreads across my face like wildfire. "My memory's a little impaired. Maybe because I was drugged."

"Bad joke." He grabs the popcorn and candy. "It's Parker."

I take our drinks and walk alongside him to theatre 3. The worn red carpet leads to an overabundance of empty seats. Are we early?

Dean looks from side to side. "Hope we can get a seat."

I chuckle. "Tenth row center is the best seat in the house."

"Really?" He walks forward and stops at row ten, holding onto our snacks for dear life.

"Yep, got the perfect distance from all sides."

"I'll take your word for it." He eases in, spilling a few kernels of popcorn on his way to the middle of the row.

I slide into the seat next to him and place his soda in the cup holder attached to the arm rest. "I find your lack of faith disturbing."

"Nice." He hands me the array of candy I ordered and sets the popcorn between us.

"Wanna share?" I rip open my box of chocolate covered peanuts and hold it out to Dean.

The lights dim, casting a golden glow around the empty theater, and illuminating Dean's face. I stare, mesmerized by his chiseled jaw and perfectly smooth skin. He shakes his head and leans in closer. My nerve endings stir, causing a series of tingles to travel from the tips of my fingers to my toes.

He tips my chin toward him and gazes into my eyes. "You're the one thing I'm not willing to share."

I squint as we walk through the door and emerge from the dark theater. Never thought I'd get the chance to see either of those movies on the big screen. Too bad I spent the last three and a half hours sitting in a dark theatre, replaying the words Dean said, over and over in my head. What was he talking about? We're just friends, sharing is required.

I blink repeatedly, finally regaining focus. Ushers and employees sweep the floor and shut down the snack bar as we make our way out of the theatre.

Dean turns toward me. "Still hungry?"

I toss my empty containers in the trash and walk toward the door. "Hell, yeah."

Dean holds open the door. "Time for part two of the celebration."

I pull my coat tight around myself and step into the frigid night. Millions of stars shine through the dark abyss of the clear sky. I breathe slowly, trying to prevent the cool air from burning my nose. I gaze around at the tranquil empty streets covered in a fresh blanket of snow, sparkling like tiny diamonds against the cool moonlight.

Dean holds out his arm. "Gerardo's is right down the block. In the mood for pizza?"

I nod and take his arm, nuzzling against him. The closer we are the more heat we generate. My heart races and blood rushes through my body. Newton seemed to miss this concept in his laws of attraction.

I walk forward, breathing deep and taking in the aroma of fresh fallen snow and Dean. Perfect combination.

I stomp my feet against the freshly shoveled concrete sidewalk in front of Gerardo's, trying to knock off the excess snow clinging to my boots. Dean eases his arm from mine and pulls open the door. I walk inside, greeted by the aroma of fresh baked bread and garlic. I inhale deeply, taking in the fresh flavors. Dean feathers his hand along the small of my back. Butterflies flutter in my stomach. He guides me to a table in the back.

I take off my coat and slide into the green leather booth. He follows suit and grabs a menu from the table.

"What's your poison?" He peruses the menu.

"Nothing sweet or cute, or called virgins." I smirk.

He glides his finger down the menu. "They've got hellfire scorchers. Right up your alley."

I kick him under the table and muffle a smile.

"What can I get you?" A dark haired girl with the body of a porn star, wearing a shirt two sizes too small, smiles. She stares at Dean tapping a pen against a notepad.

Um, hello, I'm right here. I toss my menu on the table. "We'll have a large pizza pie and two large colas."

Dean sets down the menu. "Sounds good."

Her eyes shift from Dean's fitted, gray, long-sleeved T-shirt to his deep blue eyes. "Coming right up." She takes a step back and turns away.

I look toward her, then shift my focus to Dean. "Looks like you made a new friend."

He sets his elbows on the table and leans forward. "I've got enough friends, no room for any more."

I tip my chin. "Please, anyone at your frat house would make room for her."

He shrugs. "Not interested."

"In girls." I fidget with my fingers.

"What?... No. I mean, yes. I'm interested in girls. Just not her."

My god, the guys at the frat house would line up for her. Who knows? She might even be into that kind of kinky stuff. Maybe Dean is just being polite, which would definitely not be one of the rules of the Brotherhood. How did he end up in a frat house?

"So when did you pledge Beta Omega, anyway?"

The waitress comes back with our drinks, bending over the table way further than necessary to hand Dean his. She moves slowly back, flaunting her cleavage as she turns away. "The rest will be right out."

Dean sips his drink. "Last semester."

I take a slug of my soda. "Maybe you're still transitioning into a frat boy."

He rubs his chin. "Ah, close to a compliment. I actually pledged because I plan on working for CIVAT Inc. once I get my degree. Everyone on the board is a Beta Omega Alumni. It looks good on the resume."

"Really? A whole company of fraternity brothers?" I lower my eyebrows. "Interesting, didn't know you had an ulterior motive."

He raises an eyebrow and leans forward. "There's lots you don't know about me, yet."

I tilt my head to the side. "Yet?"

He leans back and sips his soda. "This isn't the first physics test you're going to ace. Your tutor rocks." He flashes a sexy smile.

"Yeah, he's okay." My lips upturn into a smile.

"Anything else?" The waitress slides the tray of pizza and two paper plates onto the table, pulling me from my thoughts.

"Nope." Dean passes me a paper plate.

"Just let me know." She smiles, catching her bottom lip in her teeth and walks away, shaking her hips.

I roll my eyes. "Guess you're used to this from playing baseball."

He pulls a piece of pizza from the pie and slides it on my plate. "Used to what?"

I shrug. "Being the hero."

"Super Dean at your service." He grabs a slice of pizza and takes a bite.

I slap his arm playfully. It's like hitting a brick wall, pure muscle. "You know what I mean."

"I'll try to control my harem of followers." He snickers.

Who's he kidding? I know exactly how it is. Football players at our high school were like golden gods. Everyone looked up to them, wanted to date them, wanted to be them. College sports just magnify that tenfold. I've been there, done that. It's not all it's cracked up to be and repeating history isn't on my college agenda. I can't seem to stay away from the jock frat boy. It's like he's the forbidden fruit I just can't resist. *Thank god for blessing me with strong willpower.* I'll need every bit of it to steer clear of Dean Parker.

"So what about you? What do you do for fun besides chase superhero frat boys?" He raises his eyebrows.

I bite into another slice of pizza. "Nothing exciting."

He wrinkles his forehead. "Come on, everyone needs some fun."

I sip my soda. "I used to be on my high school dance team, but that seems like eons ago."

We finish the tray of pizza in Mach speed. Guess Dean fires up my appetite.

He wipes his mouth with a napkin and drops it on his plate. "You're looking at the man voted best dancer at Greenfield High. Hand to god, it's in the yearbook." He slides out of the booth and puts on his coat. "Maybe I'll show you some of my moves sometime."

I scoot out of the booth and pull on my coat, zippering it to my neck. So he wants to show me his moves. Yeah, exactly what I'm afraid of.

Millions of stars twinkle sending silver specks of light along the dark night sky on the short walk back to my apartment. A coating of snow blankets the sidewalk and roadway, sparkling against the streetlights. Tomorrow it will be a tinged with dirt and caked on the side of the road, but at the moment it's completely untouched, glowing in pristine splendor.

I slide my hands in my pockets, clenching my fingers into loose fists to conserve heat. The snow draped over the pine trees cover the benches of Lakeview Park. A gentle frigid breeze stings my cheeks. I turn toward Dean and gaze at his deep blue eyes, sparkling like silver starlight. My body instantly heats up.

He stops and meets my gaze, then bends down and grabs a mound of snow, packing into a tight ball. He takes a step back and winds his arm, throwing the snowball straight and fast. It smacks against the metal sign on the far end of the small pond near a cluster of benches, breaking off into a multitude of pieces.

He wipes his hands off on his pants. "Give it a try."

I shake my head. "No way, I throw like a girl."

His picks up a mound of snow and packs it together, forming a perfect sphere. He hands me the snowball and stands behind me, pressing his body against mine. My heartbeats thump against my chest, causing a surge of adrenaline to rush through my veins. I tremble, holding the snowball in my right hand. At least I can blame the cold for my shaky arm. He runs his hand down to my wrist and pulls it back, up toward my shoulder.

He rests his head on my shoulder and talks softly into my ear. "Pull your arm back to here and step forward at the same time you throw." He moves to the side.

Goosebumps form on my neck from his warm breath gliding against my cool skin. My stomach flutters. *Here goes nothing.* I stare at the metal No Parking sign and pull my arm back, throwing the snowball as I step forward. Tiny fragments of snow fly through the air. A direct hit.

I clap my hands and bounce up and down on my toes. "Holy crap, I actually did it. I didn't think I could hit the broad side of a barn." Dean comes over and raises his hand to give me a high five. I lunge forward and pull him into a hug, before I realize what I'm doing. My chest tightens and heat creeps across my cheek.

He wraps his arms around my waist and presses his

body against mine. I step back and ease away, dropping my arms to my sides. "We better head back, I've still got lots of physics studying to do if I plan on passing the semester."

He rubs the back of his neck and nods.

I slide my frozen hands into my pockets and hold them in tight fists. Note to self: *when I think I'm finished embarrassing myself I'm usually wrong.*

The perfect untouched blanket of snow moves into an array of chaos as we turn the corner to my apartment. My heart beats faster with each step I take forward. This walk is taking forever. If I don't get away from Dean soon, I may end up doing something else I shouldn't. I mean, we're just friends. I take a deep breath and slowly exhale as we approach my driveway.

I dig in my purse and pull out my keys. "Thanks for my victory celebration."

He places his hand in the small of my back on our way toward my steps. "First of many." His hand moves to my waist.

Summersaults take over my stomach. I step onto the first step. My boot slips along the rim of the concrete edge covered in a thin layer of ice and instantly it knocks me off balance. My hands flail through the air, desperately trying to grab onto anything.

Dean jumps into action, catching me before my head smacks against the hard sidewalk. I grab onto his sculpted bicep and pull myself to my feet.

Fire burns through my cheeks, which are no doubt fire-engine red. I drop my chin to my chest and hunch my shoulders. He lifts my chin and gazes into my eyes. My heart pounds against the walls of my chest. Electric shockwaves flows through my veins. He leans in closer. My lips part and lava flows through my body. He tucks a stray strand of hair behind my ear. "I knew you'd fall for me sooner or later." He places a soft kiss on my cheek and takes a step back, turning and walking away.

I let out the breath I'd been holding and stare until he disappears around the corner. My eyes travel along the sidewalk, stopping at the point where our two sets of footprints in the snow turn into one. My heart sinks. He's everything I vowed to stay away from, yet it kills me to let him go.

CHAPTER 5 – GIRLS JUST WANT TO HAVE FUN

I stare at the double layer chocolate cake as Lexie pushes it across the table and sets it in front of our friend Olivia. My mouth waters. Great, more things I can't resist. Looks like I'll have to kick my willpower into overdrive.

"Happy Birthday, Olivia," Lexie says, sticking a pink candle in the middle of the creamy chocolate. She unzips her purse and pulls out a Zippo lighter. Guess her theory of keeping ready in case of emergency does come in handy. She flicks her thumb and waves the flame in front of the wax wick. The candle blazes like an inferno.

"Last year as a teenager," Olivia replies with a huge smile on her face, sliding her long dark brown hair over her shoulder. She leans forward, extinguishing the candle in one quick blow.

"Make that wish count." Lexie winks and twirls her finger around her hair.

"Oh, I always make it count." Olivia dips her finger in

the chocolate and then sticks it in her mouth. "Mmm, better than sex."

I huff and roll my eyes.

"Who pissed in her Cheerios?" Olivia turns toward Lexie and wrinkles her forehead.

"Yeah, what's up with you tonight? That time of the month?" Lexie nods toward me and shovels a forkful of cake into her mouth.

"God, every time a girl isn't frolicking around like a cheerleader she must be on the rag, right? You're worse than the guys." I cut myself a mammoth piece of cake and dig in.

"Ah, I get it. Your panties are still in a bunch from your non-date." Lexie holds back a smile.

"Sorry to break it to you, but there were no panties involved in my non-date." I regret the words as soon as they leave my mouth.

Olivia and Lexie erupt into a mess of giggles.

"A panty-less non-date." Lexie smirks.

I shovel more cake into my mouth and slug down my diet cola. Thank god panties weren't involved in my non-date. It's been two days and no word from Dean. Guess I misread the signals, or he finally read mine loud and clear. Perfect example of why I need to stay away from all frat boys, even if they do seem different. Nope, same old scene; one minute you're the most interesting person in the world and the next it's like they don't even know you. Maybe now my body will listen to my brain.

I drop the menu on the table. "Let's order a bunch of appetizers and share them. Best of both worlds."

"Excellent idea." Lexie heads up to the bar and chats with our waitress, who's doing more flirting than working.

"Dean really is a great guy. I know it's none of my business but you know my boyfriend Trevor? Well he's in Beta Omega and he said Dean mentioned your non-date like, four times the other day." Olivia finishes the last forkful of cake. "Must be a record for a guy to talk about a girl that much to his brothers."

An involuntary smile creeps across my face. "He's a good friend."

She tilts her head. "You sure that's all he is?"

I throw my hands in the air. "Yes, so everyone can stop assuming it's more. We're friends, that's it, end of story."

Lexie makes her way back to our table and slides into the chair. "What did I miss?"

"Just Brooke's bitch hiccup." Olivia snickers.

A low growl escapes my throat. How ridiculous! I wouldn't be this bent out of shape if I didn't hear from any of my other friends in a few days. I've got to get it together. Plus, I'm ruining Olivia's birthday celebration. I'm the one who's a horrible friend.

"Okay, bitch episode is over. Now on to bigger and better things." I sip my soda. "What did Trevor get you for your birthday?"

Olivia shrugs. "Don't know yet." She gestures toward the door. "Looks like he just walked in…with your friend."

I turn toward the door and fidget with my fingers. Dean pulls off his hat and runs his hand through his hair, styling it in a perfect, sexy mess. My pulse rate doubles. He shrugs off his jacket, hanging it on the coat rack near the door. I stare, following the outline of his sculpted pecs flaunted by the thin material of his dark green Beta Omega T-shirt in just the right way, then move to his chiseled biceps which dance every time he moves. I nibble on my fingernails and lean back in my chair.

"Enjoy," the waitress says, breaking my trance. She sets a menagerie of plates on the table. I reach for a fry, my fingers trembling.

Olivia waves her hands in the air as if she's landing a plane. "Over here guys."

Great. I turn back toward the door and glance at Trevor, Tom, and Dean, making their way to our table. Sad excuse for a triple date on girl's night.

Olivia jumps out of her chair as Trevor approaches. He pulls her into a bear hug, his multitude of colorful tattoos peeking out from under his short-sleeved T-shirt.

"Happy Birthday, babe." Trevor drops his hands from Olivia's waist and hands her a silver box.

Olivia bounces on the balls of her feet. She slowly opens it, pulling out a gold chain with a heart attached. "Ooh, I love it! Thank you." She slams her lips against his.

"Get a room," someone from across the bar yells.

Trevor pulls away and nods. "Sounds like a plan. See you guys later." He turns toward Olivia. "The celebrating is just about to begin." He pulls her coat from the chair and holds it up.

She slips her arms inside and high tails it toward the door, turning back toward us before she leaves. "Thanks guys. I had a blast. Talk to you later." She blows us a kiss and walks out the door, almost skipping.

Leaving just the four of us—how convenient. Tom flops into Olivia's recently abandoned chair and crosses his arms over his chest, accentuating his muscles. Lexie rests her head on her chin and leans closer to him.

Amazing, how things change in an instant. And what's with the short sleeve shirts anyway? It is winter.

Dean pulls up a chair and sits next to me. "Nice, all my favorites." He winks at me and grabs a mozzarella stick, shoving it in his mouth. "How's the physics studying going?"

I squirm in my seat and stab a fried mushroom with my fork. "It's going." I breathe slowly, trying to control the thumping of my heart. Dammit, why does he have this effect on me? "What's with the summer attire?" I turn toward him and peruse the curves of his bicep, moving up to his face. My stomach flutters.

"Summer spirit week." He drags a french fry through a mound of ketchup and devours it. "Don't be surprised if you see a Beta Omega brother in a speedo."

Gross. I grimace. Hate to break it to him but no one looks good in a speedo. I mean, most women would rather see a gorgeous guy in a perfectly tailored suit than a thin layer of spandex covering his junk.

Tom turns toward Lexie. "There's an eighties band tonight. Ready to show me your moves?"

Her face turns a bright shade of crimson and she twists hair around her finger. "I'm game."

I tap my fingers against my glass of diet cola. "You'll have to watch from over there because tonight it's girl's night." I point across the room to the far corner near the bar.

Lexie shoots me a sinister gaze as if Satan himself was sitting right in front of her.

"Dammit. I could've used my wingman tonight." Dean finishes the last mozzarella stick. "My mind hasn't recouped from being stuck in a cabin for two days with no cell service. Ice fishing blows."

That's why I hadn't heard from him. Lightness fills my chest. "My wingman days are over, especially on girl's night out. Unless you want to discuss hair and nail tips."

Dean runs his hand through his hair. "I prefer the natural look."

I burst out laughing. Amazing…one minute I want him to disappear from the earth and the next I'm giggling like a flirty cheerleader.

Dean stands up from his chair and nods toward the pool table. "Ten bucks I kick your ass."

Tom's scrapes his chair along the wooden floor and stands up. "You're on." He gives Lexie a peck on the cheek and walks toward the pool table with Dean.

Lexie lowers her eyebrows and tilts her head. "Seriously. You just banished the guys from our table."

I dab my finger into some chocolate frosting and quickly suck it off. "Yep. It's girl's night, so you're stuck with me."

Lexie leans back in her chair and twirls her finger around her hair. "Listen, I get your whole anti-jock, anti-frat boy rule, but look at you. You're making yourself miserable. You like him. Go for it. What's the harm in giving it a try?"

"What's the harm in sticking your head in an alligator's mouth?" There's a damn good chance you're going to get crushed. "It'll never work. I'm not into the whole fraternity scene and besides I want a man not a party boy."

"Sometimes what you want is the opposite of what you need." She flashes a quick smile.

I exhale loudly and shove my cup toward the middle of the table. "Enough with the deep talk tonight is all about fun." I look toward the stage. "Band's almost ready, get your dancing shoes on."

Now if I could just stop her words from replaying over and over in my mind my life would be less complicated.

The drums vibrate through my chest and the screech of the guitar resonates through the crowd. Lexie and I push our way to the stage, turning sideways and elbowing through a plethora of people. I cough my way through a cloud of fruity perfume. It's like I'm at a sold out show, this place is so packed.

I glance around the jam-packed room. Dean leans against the back wall holding a pool cue in his hand. He runs his hand through his hair, and then leans forward aiming toward the cue ball. His lips upturn in a small smile as we make eye contact. Chills sweep through my body even though it's got to be at least eighty degrees in here. Is he deliberately tormenting me? Yeah, right. I'm pretty much doing that to myself.

The familiar tune of *Love is a Battlefield* blares through the speakers. Lexie and I instantly sway as if we're part of a spontaneous choreographed dance. I inadvertently break into the routine my dance team back in high school made to this song, which will never leave my brain. I close my eyes and hit every move like my body was programmed to do so. I slowly gaze at the crowd. Oh god, they had merged into a large circle with me in the center. Heat spreads across my face and my chin trembles. The crowd claps until the music stops. I cover my face with my hands and slowly drop them to my sides, walking backward until I'm pinned against the stage.

"We are *Totally Eighties* and we'll be right back after a quick break," the singer announces.

"Aren't you used to being in the spotlight from all those years of dance team?" Lexie leans against the stage next to me.

I nod. "I wasn't expecting to put on a show tonight."

"I know someone who enjoyed that show." She nudges my elbow.

I roll my eyes and fan my face with my hand. "I need a drink."

We turn sideways and slide through the crowd, getting pushed and elbowed on the way. A small area opens near the bar. A multitude of people line up, waiting for drinks.

"We'll never get a drink. The line's is at least three people deep." Lexie tries to squirm her way to the bar.

"I got this." After living in Regal Hall last semester with a room that wasn't much bigger than my closet at home, I can fit into more places than an octopus.

I slither around a scantily clad brunette and peek my head between the shoulders of two blondes wearing four-inch heels. Ah, it's not that bad. I move sideways, parallel to the bar and spot a guy in a baseball cap, taking his drink and moving to his table. Time to strike while the iron is hot. I lunge forward, grazing two people on my way and press my hands against the cool, hard, wooden bar.

A man next to me slurs his speech as he tries to order another drink. Jeez, he has one in his hand and he's hogging the bartender. Unbelievable. I pull a five-dollar bill from my pocket and place it on the bar. The bartender spots me, and comes to my aid.

"Wait your turn," the man slurs, spilling his beer all over my white shirt. His nostrils flare and his eyes protrude.

Crap. I find the place at the bar containing the mean drunk. "Sorry." I shrug.

"That's not good enough!" he screams and points his finger in my face.

I hold up my hands. "I can buy you another drink."

He shakes his head and pushes me hard, knocking me into the crowd. "You little bitches think you can do anything you want."

I crash into a high-top bar table. Pain radiates across my back. My arms tremble and my legs become weak. Does this guy seriously want to fight me? My stomach turns rock-hard and my chest tightens. He charges forward. I close my eyes and brace myself for the next blow.

Footsteps pound the wooden floor, resonating through the noisy crowd. A bead of sweat forms on my forehead and my lips tremble as I wait for the blow from the drunken man's body. I open my eyes just as Dean jumps in front of me, his hands balled into fists so tight his knuckles turn white.

"Come on, asshole." Dean steps forward and smacks his hands against the man, pushing him hard and sending him flying backwards into the line of people at the bar. "What's the matter, you only fight girls?"

The crowd of people dissipates to the sides, forming an open space for Dean and the drunk to fight. I suck in a deep breath and grip the edge of the table.

The man shakes his head and marches forward, an evil sneer gracing his face. He throws a punch at Dean. Dean ducks to the side, sending the man wobbling and struggling to keep his balance. Dean grips his fist tighter and throws an uppercut to his stomach. The man bends over, gasping for breath.

"Hell, no. You don't get away that easy." Dean grabs the back of the man's hair with one hand, pulls up his head, and punches him hard in the face with the other hand.

The man's face jerks to the side, some spit and blood fly out. Dean grabs him by his red and white flannel shirt, shaking him. "No one ever touches her. Got it?" Dean says through gritted teeth.

The man's head wobbles from side to side and his eyes

roll to the back of his head.

Lexie and Tom break through the crowd and run up to me. "Are you okay?" Lexie gives me a hug.

I nod.

Tom pulls Dean off the man, just as the bartender steps up to them. "Am I going to need to call the police?" he asks.

Tom holds up his hands. "No sir, we're leaving."

Dean runs his hands through his hair, and grips the back of his neck. I stare at the peaks and valleys of his biceps, bursting through his skin as he moves. My heart beats in my ears as hot lava flows through my veins. Dean brings his hands down and glances at his knuckles, the skin broken and tinged with blood.

Dear god, he's never looked sexier. My brain shuts down and every ounce of willpower keeping me away from him disappears. Every doubt, every fear, instantly fades as if it never existed. I lunge forward and slam my lips into his, weaving my fingers in the back of his hair. He wraps his arms around my waist, pulling me close to his body. A roar of clapping erupts throughout the bar, growing faint as I lose myself in this perfect moment.

CHAPTER 6 — HANDCUFF PARTY?

I close my physics book and turn toward Dean. "Let me get this straight. Not only do you want me to come to a frat party, but you want me to be handcuffed to you the whole time?"

He rubs the back of his neck. "Yeah. I get it, it sounds crazy."

"Um, just a little." I crinkle my eyebrows and tap my pen against the table of the library.

"I'm kinda running the party." He bounces his knee.

Great. Despite my immense hatred for all things frat related, there's no way in hell I'm letting some other girl be handcuffed to Dean all night. Looks like I've got to suck it up. I sigh heavily and tap my foot. "Fine, but find me something non-alcoholic to drink so we don't have a repeat of last time."

He raises his right hand. "You got it. And I promise, nothing kinky with the handcuffs."

"Then never mind." I blush.

"Be careful what you wish for." He winks.

"Shhh." A girl across from us shoots us a dirty look and points at the Keep Quiet sign hung on the library wall near the bookshelf.

I chuckle. Maybe moving our physics study sessions to the library wasn't the best idea. "Guess we better get out of here before she has us handcuffed." I hold up my wrists.

Hmm. So what does one wear to a party where the main focus is to be handcuffed to another person? The silver rod screeches as the hangers slide along the metal at Mach speed. Everything's different now. Does he expect me to stay? I nibble at my fingernails. Not sure I'm ready for that yet. No need to relive my senior year of high school. I'm still getting used to the idea I'm actually dating…a party guy. I grimace at the words running through my mind.

I close my eyes and take a deep breath. Okay, time to focus. I glide my fingers along the fabric of at least fifty articles of clothing and stop at my navy V-neck fitted shirt I usually save for the bar. I pull down my plastic tote of

Halloween costumes from the top shelf of my closet and take the sheriff pin off my sexy cop costume from last year. Perfect. I'm bound to see a plethora of half-naked girls dressed as cops or criminals. I affix the shiny silver pin to my shirt and grab a pair of dark-wash skinny jeans along with my black high-heeled ankle boots.

Lexie peeks her head into the doorway. "Ready for tonight?"

"Ready as I'll ever be." I slide on my jeans and pull my shirt over my head.

She walks inside my room and plops on my bed. "Sheriff, nice." She gives me a thumbs-up.

"You wearing that?" I glance at her sweat pants and oversized T-shirt.

"Yeah, I'm pretending I was arrested at a twenty-four hour department store."

"Hmm, some slippers and you can pull it off." I smirk.

She throws a pillow at me. "I'm thinking tights and a sweater dress." She scoots up on my bed and sits Indian style. "So you finally gave in to the dark side. And all it took was free tutoring, a non-date, and a bar fight."

I smear on some candy-apple red lip-gloss and smack my lips together. "I like to play hard to get." I wink.

She shakes her head and hops off the bed. "For the

record, I think this is going to be an awesome semester for us."

I give my hair a few final touch-ups. "Yeah, first I get drugged, now I'll be in handcuffs. Can't wait to see what's in store for me next."

She leans against the doorway. "FYI, never ask that question." She disappears down the hall.

I apply some black mascara and stand back, staring in the mirror. My eyes sweep over my navy V-neck clinging to my body with the shiny silver badge pinned above my right breast. Why do I feel like I just regressed back to the days of careless partying and hooking up with god knows who? My heart flutters. I take a few steps back and sit on the edge of my bed. There's no way I'm turning into that girl again.

A soft knocking pulls me out of my thoughts as Lexie taps on the door frame. She tips her head and scrunches her eyebrows. "You okay?" She comes over and joins me on the bed.

I nod. "Yep, just thinking of everything I need for tonight."

Lexie pulls me into a side hug. "I think that outfit will cover all your bases."

I look down at my V-neck. Maybe it is a little deep.

Lexie stands and looks me up and down. "Where's the sheriff? I think someone needs to be arrested for indecent exposure." She laughs.

I cross my arms over my chest. Dammit, that makes it worse. I shoot her a death glare.

She takes a step back and puts her hands on her hips. "So, what do you think?" She twirls around, showing off her purple sweater dress and black tights."

I rub my chin. "I think I may be walking home alone. Tom won't need the handcuffs to be stuck to your side tonight."

"Who knows? Maybe we'll be walking home together in the morning." She raises her eyebrows and twirls her hair around her finger.

Not sure I'm ready for that yet. I mean, sure I've been with more guys then I care to remember but Dean is just…different. I guess I'll just play it by ear.

Lexie nibbles on her fingernails. "Oh crap. What if I'm handcuffed to someone else? It's all random, right?"

I stand up and grab my purse from my dresser. "The sheriff can help you out." I flash my badge and swing my purse around my shoulder. Never in a million years would I let my best friend be handcuffed to some random loser while the guy she likes is handcuffed to another girl.

Time to head to the frat house—something I said I'd never do again. What other promises will I break tonight?

I slam the door, sending a gust of frigid air through the foyer. Dean adjusts his oversized sunglasses, which makes him look like Ponch from CHiPs, and slides them up onto his head. Well, a much hotter, sexier version. I stare at his muscles moving underneath his fitted T-shirt. He fidgets with the door lock and snaps the deadbolt shut.

Dean rubs his hands together and joins me at the 'arraignment table'. He grabs the megaphone from under the table and stands on his chair. "Rules are as follows: babes write their name on a pink slip of paper, dudes on a blue piece. Hand them over to Sheriff Brooke and we'll get this party started." He jumps down, tossing the megaphone to the side and pulls out a tote of handcuffs.

A mob of people rush toward the table, setting their drinks aside to write their names on the small slips of paper. I lunge backward, pushing myself against the back of my chair to avoid being mauled to death in the struggle to grab a pen. Seriously? These people are like crazed lunatics. Don't they realize they may be signing up for a night of hell? I mean, what if they're tethered to someone they despise?

I slide two large, empty industrial mayonnaise jugs Dean managed to snag from the cafeteria toward the edge of the table, placing one by the blue slips of paper and one by the pink slips. "Drop your papers in the jugs when you're done."

Tanya Layton folds her pink slip of paper in half and sets her elbows on the table. She leans in front of Dean, holding her arms tight to her body to push her cleavage in his face. Her breasts are about to pop out of the scoop neck of her low cut red shirt.

"Hope I get cuffed to you." She blows Dean a kiss.

I clench my fists and jump out of my chair. Who the hell does she think she is? I mean, hello, I'm right here. Maybe she can work her magic on Dr. Jenners but her little miss sultry routine isn't going to work this time.

I place my palms on the table and lean toward her. My nostrils flare as I speak. "The sheriff will do the pairing tonight." I lean back and flash my badge toward her.

She huffs and waves her hand. "Whatever."

Dean runs his tongue along his lips, muffling a smile. "The sheriff is pretty bad-ass."

I slide back into my chair and turn toward Dean.

"Think of *Fargo*. You know, minus the pregnant."

"Nice…and a little scary." He winks.

The crowd dissipates, leaving a few people who quickly pop their names in the jars. Looks like we're ready to go. I grab a piece of blue paper and a piece of pink paper and scribble our names on them.

I fold the papers in half and turn toward Dean. "Looks like we've got our first set of victims."

He places a finger on each piece of paper and slides them along the table in front of him. His lips upturn into a small smile as his eyes glance across the letters. "Awesome, my partner in crime." He grabs a set of the novelty handcuffs and clips one cuff to his wrist.

He reaches for my hand and slowly grazes his fingertips along my wrist. My heart pounds against my chest like a jackhammer. He clicks the cuff shut, making sure it's not too tight. Perfect fit. He turns toward me and we stand face to face. His eyes lock onto mine and I'm lost in the sea of deep blue. The world fades away for split second and nothing else exists, it's just me and Dean.

"Who's next?" a guy yells through the room.

I jerk my head and blink repeatedly, pulling myself back into reality. Dean and I both reach for a bucket in opposite directions with our free hands. The handcuffs pull us back toward each other. I lose my balance from the force and slam into Dean's arm.

"You okay?"

I nod. "Never better."

I hand Dean the two slips of paper I've confiscated and held in my pocket. He bends down and picks up the megaphone. "Tom Johnson and Lexie Waters."

I pull the tote of handcuffs onto the table with my free hand. Thank god the same key opens all the cuffs. If not, there'd be no guarantees of finding the right one after hours of drinking. Dean and I work together with our cuffed hand and clip the handcuffs onto Lexie and Tom.

"Thanks, sheriff." Lexie winks at me.

"My job is to uphold justice, ma'am." I wave as she and Tom walk away into the kitchen.

We go through the entire bucket of names and handcuff everyone together. Ah, Tanya Layton. I hand the slip of paper to Dean and lean over to see who her man is for the night. I scan the letters written in black ink. Huh, Randy Andrews. Good luck dealing with the ten gallons of cologne he uses to cover the smell of pot clinging to every article of clothing he wears. A sinister smile graces my face.

"Your sentence lasts until 2 a.m. Beer Pong

tournament in an hour." He drops the megaphone and tugs at our cuffs. He moves his wrist around the cuff and holds my hand. "Want a drink?"

I tilt my head and look up at him. "Hell no."

He walks around the table, guiding me with him. "Don't worry, your wingman has you covered." We walk along the dingy green carpet, swaying between the crowd of cuffed couples to the kitchen. He pulls open the refrigerator door and hands me a can of diet cola.

I take the cool can and lean in closer to Dean. "Super Dean to the rescue." I give him a quick peck on the cheek.

His cheeks turn a slight shade of pink. "All in a day's work."

He grabs a plastic cup and we make our way to the keg. I set down my soda and push the button on the tap. This whole party is almost a weird experiment on teamwork in a social setting. Someone should write their thesis on handcuff parties.

We take our drinks and head to the study off the kitchen where he saved me from a drunken loser the first time we met. We plop down on an empty space of the burgundy couch. I sink into the cushion and peruse the Ping-Pong table set up with small white balls and a multitude of red plastic cups. Guess the tournament takes place here.

Dean sips his beer. "Best sheriff in all of Lakeview."

I chuckle. "All in a day's work." I sip my diet cola and set the can on small table next to me.

Dean plucks his sunglasses off his head and tosses them on the table. "Everyone may try to escape when Tom starts the speeches."

"Huh? There's speeches at these parties?" I rub my chin.

"Sad but true. Tom has to give this speech on how Beta Omega coined the term handcuff party. He's in charge until our Prez, Jesse, gets back next semester." He reaches for his beer and takes a sip. "It's all bullshit. Every fraternity says they created beer pong, and toga parties, and handcuff parties."

Great. Maybe this is why they don't serve non-alcoholic drinks at these parties. "I could always call in and say you kidnapped me."

"Not sure the scholarship board will like that one."

I look down at the rough scabs on his knuckles. My stomach hardens. The scholarship committee probably wouldn't be too thrilled with Dean getting into bar fights either. Thank god no one pressed charges. Ugh, what would've happened if he wasn't there? My chest tightens. I still can't believe he risked getting kicked off the team for me. Looks like I'll have to get extremely creative to make it up to him.

"Did you always love baseball?"

He grabs his cup of beer. "Ever since I could walk. Plus there's not a hell of a lot to do in Iowa, mostly farms."

Yeah, I know the feeling. "There's got to be some excitement."

He shrugs. "John Wayne was from Iowa." He lowers his eyes and purses his lips. "A man's got to do what a man's got to do."

I let out a short burst of laughter, almost spitting on Dean. "You sure acting isn't your calling?"

"Ever notice my close shave?"

Just about every time I look at you. "Yeah."

He raises his eyebrows. "In Iowa, it's illegal for a mustached man to kiss a woman in public." He raises his right hand. "Hand to god."

I laugh and sip my diet cola. "Sounds like my kind of place."

He sips his beer. "Who knows, maybe you'll see it sometime."

A series of tingles jolt through my body. Never know—maybe I will meet Dean's family sometime. I mean, assuming I can get through tonight. I stare at his smooth skin and chiseled jaw line, his cheeks tinged with just the slightest pink hue leading up to those deep blue eyes you can get lost in forever.

"Let's get ready to rumble. Beer Pong battle!" Tom screams through the megaphone, breaking my trance.

Lexie tiptoes on her high-heeled boots trying to keep up with Tom. She stands in front of the beer pong table, staggering and swaying. Oh god, she's actually playing.

I stand up and turn toward Dean, gently tugging on our cuffs. "I've gotta be her cheerleader."

He rises from the couch and stands next me. "I'll give the play-by-play."

We walk to the middle of the table and Dean takes the megaphone from Tom. "Round one. Tom and Lexie versus Olivia and Trevor."

Lexie rocks on her heels, swaying back and forth like she's on an Alaskan fishing boat. Seriously? How the hell did she get wasted this fast?

"You can't be drunk already."

She twirls her hair around her finger with her free hand and lets out a slight giggle. "Not drunk, buzzed. We were doing shots with Trevor and Olivia."

Well, this round won't last long, especially with

Lexie's superb drinking skills. I look over at Dean and shake my head. He shrugs and holds the megaphone to his mouth. "Rules are, no bouncing. The ball has to go directly into the cup. Ready... Go."

Lexie tosses the ball forward with all her might. It hits me square in the nose. I grimace. Oh, she is going to pay for that one. I rub my nose with my free hand.

"Oops," she mutters and she grips the end of the table for balance.

Tom tosses two balls, landing each one in a cup as if he's a professional in the sport. Olivia and Trevor make all four balls. Tom pushes two cups of beer toward Lexie and takes two cups for himself.

"Bottoms up." Tom raises his cups toward Lexie.

"I think she's had enough." I step to the side, as far as my cuffs will allow, and hold her arm.

"Rules are rules!" Tom shouts and slams both beers, crushing the cups.

Now I remember why I hate frat parties. Nothing but testosterone- and alcohol-filled events in which men act like cavemen and women demean themselves to allowing it. Please let me make it through this unscathed.

Lexie gestures for me with her finger. "You got to uncuff me," she slurs, "before I puke all over."

I dig in my pocket for one of the spare keys and quickly unlatch Tom and Lexie's handcuff.

"Hey, what gives?" Tom snarls.

"It's this or puke all over you." I scowl. He's kind of an asshole. What does she see in him anyway?

Tom raises his hand, the open cuff hanging down, and grabs the megaphone. "My partner bailed. Who wants the job?"

Tanya Layton rises from the chair on the other side of the room. She raises her hands, no cuffs. I sweep my eyes over the room. That sneaky bitch. Randy leans on the chair, handcuffed to the spokes. His eyes are only small slits and his mouth has fallen open, exposing a small amount of drool.

"Alright a taker." Tom slams a beer and hooks the cuff on Tanya.

She runs her nose along his cheek, planting a small kiss near his ear. What a whore! Tom grabs her by the waist and hoists her up on the beer pong table. The cups slide along the table, beer swooshing over the rim and spilling onto the green surface. He slams his lips against hers and reaches up to fondle her breast.

Lexie walks in at that exact moment. She gasps and covers her face with her hands. "Bastard!" she screams.

Her hands slowly slide down, exposing her tear-filled eyes and red cheeks. She marches forward, grabs a cup of beer, and throws it, spilling the liquid all over Tanya's white shirt and Tom's face. Lexie storms out of the room, tears running down her cheeks.

I rush ahead, pulling Dean along. "I've got see if she's okay." Dean stumbles forward and trips over the megaphone, knocking into me on his way down. We both plummet to floor, my chin slides along the filthy carpet. Fire rips along my skin. *Dear God, please let my skin be intact.* Who knows what type of new and undiscovered bacteria live on this floor? I've got more important things to worry about at the moment. Poor Lexie.

Dean hops to his feet and pulls me up, ending my struggle. I continue moving my head from side to side to try and catch a glimpse of where she went. A flash of her long-brown curls and purple sweater rush through the door, slamming it hard. I lunge forward into a sprint, pulling Dean behind me.

"I don't work out this hard at practice. Maybe coach should hire you." He jogs by my side, quickly catching up. White vapors pour from his mouth.

"Motivation is the key...there she is." We spot Lexie and catch up to her. The frigid air blows through the quiet night. I slow to a trot, shivering.

She slows to a fast walk, wiping a few tears away from her eyes with one hand and clenches a cup of beer with the other. "What an asshole."

"Scum of the earth," I say, pulling her into a side hug, my teeth chattering.

Dean walks alongside, silent. Clearly guys have no clue what to say at times like these. I've got to give him a break, Tom although an asshole, is still his fraternity brother. It's not like Dean is going to go bashing him with the girls.

"I hope he fucking rots in hell, and that slut Tanya can go with him." She sips her beer.

Flashing hues of blue and red illuminate the night sky and a blaring siren cuts through the air. Crap. The cops. My pulse rate doubles. Memories rush through my head like a ton of bricks. Last time I was in a situation like this, Mom had to pick me up from the precinct after Kayley's mega beach party got busted. Not a memory I'd like to relive.

"Ma'am, what's in the cup?" An officer pulls alongside us in his car, flashing a light at Lexie.

She shrugs and wipes a stray tear away from her face.

"It's mine, officer." Dean stops and walks up to the police cruiser.

What the hell is he doing? He just said the scholarship committee won't tolerate any criminal activity. Is he insane? He's got everything to lose.

The officer steps out of the car and shines his flashlight in Dean's face. Dean squints, temporarily blinded.

The officer moves the light down to our handcuffs. "Can you explain this?"

"Yes, officer. We're coming from a handcuff party at Beta Omega. I was just making sure the girls made it home safe."

The officer shakes his head. "I'm sorry, there are open container laws. I'll have to take you in."

"No." I stand in front of Dean. I can't let him take the blame for this. I stare up at the cop, my heart pounding like a jackhammer. What the hell am I doing? This is how people end up on the news, beaten by cops. I step to the side, frozen. "Can't we just get a warning? We'll never do it again. Please, just give us a break." My eyes well up with tears.

The officer shakes his head. "I'm sorry, he's coming with me."

The officer twists our novelty handcuffs and slides them off. He grabs Dean by the arm and shoves him in the back of the cruiser. I cover my mouth with my hands and take in small breaths between gasps. A river of tears flow down my cheeks as our eyes lock through the window. The police cruiser drives away, taking my superhero to be tried for a crime he didn't commit. Typical, like a million love stories through the ages. I guess it is kind of romantic. I wipe my cheeks and let the cold breeze dry my eyes. Sometimes the hero is the one who needs saving and I'm off to the rescuc.

CHAPTER 7 — STAY

I bounce my knee so fast my whole body trembles. I lean back in the hard plastic chair of campus police headquarters. Guess I was so preoccupied with the shit storm happening in front of me that I didn't notice the huge Lakeview U emblem on the police car. Thank god it wasn't the actual police department. Tonight would be going a whole lot different. I nibble at my nails and stare at the large clock on the wall of the small room. The second hand ticks slowly, almost as if it's going backward. I scan the bright white walls adorned with a poster of Stevie Wonder that reads "I'd rather drive than get in a car with someone who's been drinking" and a few pictures of the campus police officers. I set my feet flat on the tan tiles and gaze at the campus officer, sitting in a large mahogany desk in front of me, scribbling on some papers.

I replay the scene in my mind over and over again. If Dean knew these were the campus police he would've never even stopped. There's no way he knew or he would've let them just take Lexie home, or at least let her sober up in headquarters. No, he was willing to lay his whole scholarship on the line just to protect me and Lexie. What was he thinking? I'm torn between hugging and slapping him when I see him.

The officer fits the paperwork into a manila folder and closes it. He glides his chair along the tiles and rises up like a mighty oak. "He's on his way out."

I stand up and fidget with my fingers. "Thanks."

The officer shakes his head and sits back down, grabbing another paper from his desk.

I stare at the door in front of me, willing it to open. Footsteps thump toward me, getting louder with each passing moment. The large gray door swings open and a jolt of electricity shoots through my body.

Dean runs his hand through his hair, tousling it into that perfect mess. He drops his hands to his sides and walks forward. He's never looked sexier than he does right at this moment.

"I'm all yours." He winks and flashes a sexy half-smile.

My eyes well up with tears and I laugh at the same time, lunging forward and wrapping my arms around his neck. "What were you thinking, you goof?" Probably not the best reaction. I step backward and raise my head, meeting his gaze.

"That's no way to thank your wingman." He wraps his arm around me and walks forward. "I've had enough of the precinct." He waves at the cops. "Later guys."

They nod. "Good luck this season," the officer behind the desk says. He looks up for a split second, then returns to his paperwork.

I hand Dean an oversized hoodie I won at my last dance team competition. One size fits all, plus it's the only thing at my apartment that has a chance of fitting him. When he used his one phone call on me I had to get to him as fast as I could. Besides, if anyone can pull off hot pink, it's him.

He takes the hoodie and holds it up. "Just my color." He slips it on and grazes his fingers over mine, gripping my hand. We huddle together and walk into the cold winter night. A gust of frigid air along with a few stray snowflakes caresses my skin, sending goose bumps throughout my body. Dean presses against me. My stomach drops to the ground.

"At least my apartment's only a block away." I trudge forward leaning into Dean, trying to soak up the warmth from his hot body.

"Guess I'm heading back with no cuffs, no girl, and a

pink hoodie. Just how I imagined the night would go." He squeezes me tighter.

I look up at him and shake my head. My teeth chatter and white vapors escape from my mouth. "You're staying with me."

He scrunches his eyebrows and slightly jerks his head back. "At your apartment?"

I nod. "It's a rule, I have to monitor anyone I bust out of jail."

A wide smile creeps across his face. "You're the sheriff."

I smirk. Weaving my arm with his, we make our way back to my apartment.

My hand trembles as I jiggle the key in the lock. With a soft click it gives, opening the door. My pulse skyrockets; no going back now.

Dean smacks his feet against the doormat, shaking loose snow from his black boots. "Want me to take them off?"

Lava flows through my veins. "Leave them in here so they don't freeze. Unless you want high-heeled boots to go with your pink hoodie on the walk back tomorrow." I toss the keys on the counter.

"Wouldn't be the first time." He snickers and sets his boots on the throw carpet in the kitchen, closing the door behind him.

I open the fridge. "Big decision. Sweet girly wine, diet soda, or pink champagne." I turn toward Dean.

"Pink's my color." He pulls the hoodie over his head, catching his T-shirt.

My eyes lock onto the hem of the shirt on its journey over the treacherous terrain of Dean's abs. Sweet Jesus he's got an eight-pack. My lips part and heat floods through my body, from my head to my toes. My nerve endings stir and tingle. I follow the fabric over his pecs. He's so much more impressive than I gave him credit for. Who knew he was hiding a body that should be chiseled in stone underneath all those clothes? My hand releases the refrigerator door and it slams shut.

My eyes glue to the fabric as he pulls it down over each peak and valley slowly. My mouth falls open and I stare in awe.

"See something you like?" He flashes a sexy half-smile and pulls his T-shirt down.

Caught red-handed. Warmth spreads across my cheeks

like wildfire. I take out the bottle of pink champagne and hold it by its neck. "Making sure there's no weapons on you."

He holds out his hands. "Maybe you should frisk me."

Oh God. There's no way on earth I can act like one of those flirty frat-party girls, especially completely sober. Sure, I've done it a hundred times drunk but that was another time, another me. I bite at my lip. *Please don't let me ruin this.*

I shake my head and take two clear plastic cups from the stack on the countertop. "Follow me, if you know what's good for you." I wink and walk into the hallway.

Okay, maybe not the best way to get him into my bedroom but I've got to be realistic. With my luck, Lexie will wake up for a glass of water in her underwear and freak if she sees Dean. It's not like I can warn her. She's passed out and three sheets to the wind.

My muscles quiver and my stomach rolls. I step onto the soft tan carpet of my bedroom. Dean follows closely behind. I set the champagne and cups down on my desk and wipe my palms against my jeans.

He looks around at my collage of pictures with a few of my medals earned from dance competitions hanging around the frames. He walks toward them and holds the metal medallion. "You must be good."

Lifting my shoulders, I shrug, "I was okay."

"Was?"

I pop open the champagne and pour us two glasses, handing one to Dean. I take a sip, the bubbles tickling my nose. "I'm done competing."

He scrunches his eyebrows and opens his mouth, but quickly closes it.

No way in hell am I getting into this conversation now. I've got to move things in a different direction. I take his free hand and guide him to my bed. I sit on the edge and scooch up. He plops down next to me, sloshing champagne to the rim of his cup.

"I never said thank you for covering for me and Lexie." I sip my champagne and fidget.

"All in a day's work." He sips his champagne and grimaces. "Ugh, it's like battery acid mixed with sugar. Girls like this crap?"

I let out a slight chuckle. "Want something else?" I slug the rest of my champagne and toss my cup in the trashcan.

He shakes his head and sets his cup down on the nightstand. "The slammer sobered me up."

My lips press into a white slash and I fold my arms

across my chest. "What the hell were you thinking?"

"Huh?" He crinkles his eyebrows and tilts his head.

"You're unbelievable." My head shakes while my eyes roll. "What if they were real cops?"

He shrugs. "Then I guess I'd be screwed."

That's it? "Don't you care about the future?"

His body tenses and he glares with hard eyes. "You're not great at thank you's."

I throw my hands in the air. "You could have lost your scholarship, got kicked off the team, and had a police record. Don't you think before you do things?"

He shakes his head and mutters something under his breath. "Yeah, and we could've all been cited for having an open container. Doubt real cops would dig the whole handcuff deal." He locks his eyes with mine, his face flushed. "Don't you get it? All I think about is you." He runs his hand through his hair and exhales loudly. "You're in my head every second of every day. No way in hell I'd let you go down. Not tonight, not ever."

The heat of a thousand suns radiates through my body. He's willing to risk everything just to protect me? I leap on top of him, slamming my lips onto his. The force knocks his body against the bed, pinning him underneath me.

He freezes for a second then glides his fingers along

the bottom hem of my shirt. Slowly pulling it up, he runs his fingertips along the curve of my back. No holding back now. Jolts of electric energy flows through my veins. Oh my god, this is really happening. I lift myself until I'm straddling him and hold my arms in the air. He rises up to a sitting position and slides off my shirt, tossing it to the floor. Our lips break for a split second as the fabric moves over my head, then lock back together as if they can't stand to be apart. How did I manage to resist him this long? I lower my arms and trace my fingertips along the thin fabric of his T-shirt, gliding them along the peaks and valleys of his back. God, I need him, now. I grip the hem and pull it hard, up and over his head, flinging it into oblivion. I pull back and catch my breath, admiring the view. Amazing, that body looks better every time I see those sculpted biceps and eight-pack abs; pure perfection at its finest.

He eases his fingers underneath the straps of my bra, slowly lowering them down my shoulders. He places soft kisses along my neck. Adrenaline flows through my veins, pushing my body into overdrive. He reaches around and unhooks my bra with a snap of his fingers. I let out a soft moan as he slides his hands forward, cupping my breasts with his calloused hands. The sensation sends shockwaves through my core.

Dean shifts his weight and leans over, nudging me down against the soft purple comforter. He hovers above me. My focus shifts to the eyes that can pierce my soul. I can't take any more; I need to feel him. I flatten my hands up his back, pulling him close against me. My heart stammers and my breathing turns into panting. He moves his hand down my breast and shifts his body to the side, unbuckling my jeans with his nimble fingers.

A shiver that brings pure pleasure sweeps through my body like a tidal wave. He slides his fingers along my belly, slowly moving his fingertips in small circles along the edge of my jeans. Is he deliberately teasing me? My heart pounds and every inch of my body tingles. His fingers creep down, making their way underneath the black lace panties that I bought just in case. He fits his fingers inside me, and rolls my body toward his. I let out a slight moan as he pleasures my most sensitive areas. Ah, baseball players really do have gifted hands.

No need to be selfish. I slide my hand over his eight-pack abs and follow the line of the sexy V that seems to point to the direction of the promised land. I yank at the button, pulling it open in one sweep. His muscles tense. My turn to give him a taste of his own medicine. I glide my hand underneath his jeans and boxers, the zipper gives way as I move down. I rub my hands against his length. Impressive. He gasps and exhales loudly.

He pulls his hand away from my most sensitive areas and grips my wrist, stopping me from touching him. "You sure?"

I slide my hand up to his heart and nod.

He hovers over me and tugs on my jeans, taking them, along with my underwear, off in one quick motion. I arch my back to help him with the journey. He stares at me, focused, as if it's the last play of a big game and he's going for the grand slam. He reaches into his back pocket and pulls out his wallet, slipping a condom from the inside fold and setting it next to us on the bed. He wiggles out of his jeans and kicks them off, along with his boxers.

Every cell in my body aches for him. He grabs the silver wrapper from the bed and tears it with his teeth, quickly unrolling the sheath over himself. A gasp escapes me and I realize that everything is about to change in one split second. My body trembles as he lowers himself over me. I breathe deep, trying to control my heart rate. What am I thinking? No reason to hold back now. I part my legs sliding my thighs against his hips and pull him close. He slowly fits himself into me. I gasp as he fills me completely, pressing against every cell inside my core.

We move in a slow, steady motion, both of us mimicking the other's movements. My breathing rate triples and my heart slams against the walls of my chest. I dig my fingers in his back, the passion building quickly. He thrusts inside me, slow and deep. A surge of electricity flows through every ounce of my being. I gasp and my toes curl. My body ignites, sending me into another dimension.

He moans as I press my fingernails into his back, releasing my built-up passion. He moves faster, thrusting himself inside me hard. I slam my body into his, desperately trying to give him the same pleasure. Oh, he definitely deserves to be pleasured. He grabs my hips and pulls them toward him, holding me tight to his impressive length. I grind against him, back and forth. He lets out a loud groan and explodes inside me, gripping my hips tight.

I press my head into the sheets and he collapses on top of me, slowly catching his breath. He props himself up so we're face-to-face and tucks a few stray strands of hair behind my ear. "You're insanely amazing."

Heat creeps across my face, along with a smile. "Right back atcha."

He rolls over onto his back and takes a few deep breaths. "Be right back." He kisses my cheek and hops off the bed, pulling on his boxers.

"First door on the left," I say as he heads out of the bedroom, disappearing into the dim lit hallway.

I sit up and cover myself with the silky lavender sheet. Insanely amazing doesn't begin to explain what just occurred. That was...otherworldly. I run my hand through my slightly tangled hair and gaze into the mirror of my triple dresser. Please tell me that's not who I think it is staring back at me.

CHAPTER 8 — BE MINE

I follow every rule of Lakeview U; I do everything I'm told to prevent chaos from raining down on my future, but Dean Parker has me breaking my own rules. It's like someone has snatched my brain and turns it into mush every time he's near me. My stomach knots and tightens. Everything was fine; my life was plotted into a perfect outline of success. Now it's spinning into a vortex of...god knows what. When did I lose control? I cover my face with my hands and drag them down to my chin. I look around the floor at our random articles of clothing tossed around in wild rage of unbridled passion. Flashbacks of hook-ups underneath the bleachers after my high school football games, backseat rendezvous, and glimpses of waking up with guys I hardly knew run through my mind like a freight train. A painful tightness forms in my chest, almost suffocating me. I struggle to suck in a breath.

I swallow hard and take a deep breath. Not this time. That girl is gone and Dean isn't some random hook-up. Now if I can just convince myself there's a chance this won't go up in flames. Not that I could resist the fire.

Dean walks back through the doorway running a hand through his hair. My hands drop to my sides, falling onto the silky sheets. My eyes scan every inch of his scorching hot body. I follow the lines of his muscles, dancing in perfect choreographed motion with every movement. Heat rushes through my body like a raging inferno. Self-control where are you?

He slides onto the bed and scoots over next to me, propping himself on his elbow. "Maybe we should fight more often." He smirks.

"Or maybe I shouldn't let my emotions get the best of me." I pull the sheet up, covering as much of my body as possible, and turn toward him, fidgeting with my fingers.

"You okay?" He lightly runs his fingers along my arm.

I nod. "I'm just not…this kind of girl any more."

He wrinkles his eyebrows and slightly jerks his head back. "What kind of girl?"

I drop my eyes to the purple sheets and sigh. "I'm afraid I'm on a backwards path."

He lifts my chin, locking his deep blue eyes with mine. "Fear is the path to the dark side." He winks.

"Some places are darker than others."

He has no idea how dark life can get. How can he? I

lean back and turn my head away from him, trying to hold in the tears.

Dean eases forward and trails his fingertips down my arm into my hand, interlocking his fingers with mine. "Brooke."

I reach down and snag my T-shirt off the floor, quickly pulling it over my head. I flick off a stray tear from my cheek before turning toward him. I try my best to form my lips into a smile, a small attempt to hide the pain. "I'm sorry."

He runs his thumb across my fingers. "I'm not...well, except for you crying after sex. I'm hoping they're tears of joy though. Right?" He nudges my arm playfully.

I let out a slight giggle, desperately trying to prevent any more tears from spewing out. Amazing, he can make me laugh even when I dredge up my worst possible memory. I look down at our interlocked hands. I pull my hand away and shift my body toward him, so we're face-to-face. My stomach drops to the floor and my muscles quiver. "Look, I really like you, but."

He shakes his head and exhales loudly. "It's because of Beta Omega, right?" He rubs the back of his neck and his lips press into a line. "Unbelievable. No matter what I do or say you can't get past that?" He sighs letting out a slight laugh. "Girls are way worse than guys."

Dammit. This went so much better in my head. I run my hands over my face and through my hair. "Let me explain myself before you walk out of here and never speak to me again." I take a deep breath and swallow hard. "I'm just....not what you're looking for. I'll never be one of those girls who hangs out at parties with handcuffs or god knows what else. I was once. Not anymore."

He huffs and runs a hand through his hair. "I'll decide what I'm looking for. Just so you know, it's not some girl to hang all over me at parties." His cheeks turn crimson. "Wait, what are you talking about...anymore?"

I fidget with my fingers and stare into his eyes, which are much colder than they were a few minutes ago. "About a year and a half ago, I lost my Dad...stomach cancer." I swallow hard. "I was completely blindsided when we found out, but hearing the news he only had one month left with us if we were lucky, was like being flung off of an airplane into a volcano." My stomach rolls and a dull ache forms in the back of my throat.

Dean's eyes narrow. He places his hand on my thigh, rubbing his thumb along my skin. "I'm sorry." He raises his eyes to look back into mine.

I let out a deep breath. "Worst day of my life. Anyway,

I just couldn't handle it. I didn't care. Not about school, not about my future, not about myself. I guess it was the easiest way for me to deal with the heartbreak."

My lip quivers as I try to get the words out. "I disappointed him," I whisper. A stray tear falls down my cheek. "Turned into everything he raised me not to be." I wipe the tear away and blink repeatedly, trying to prevent any more from escaping. "I got wasted every day. I mean wasted until I couldn't feel anything. Hooked up with random guys just to feel good for a few minutes. I was a total disaster." Another tear rolls down my cheek.

Dean moves forward and wipes it away. "Hey, we've all got our crosses to bear."

I shake my head and cover my face with my hands, slowly dropping them back to my sides. "I just can't be that girl any more. The one who wakes up after being drugged at a frat house, moderates handcuff parties, bails guys out at the police station...or campus police station and hooks up with no commitment. It's like I'm on my way back to that place....to becoming a disappointment." A flush of heat spreads across my cheeks.

Dean grabs my hand pulling me so close our lips are almost touching. "Then you're the perfect disappointment." He lifts my hand to his lips, placing a soft kiss on my knuckles, "And this wasn't a random hook-up." He brushes his lips across mine. "I want you and only you and not just for one night."

My heart thrashes against my chest and electricity surges through my body. *Dean wants me?* Just the thought of being Dean's, sends butterflies fluttering through the depths of my soul. He knows about the skeletons of my past. Is it even possible for a relationship with him to work? Guess I'll never know unless I try and Dean is worth trying for. I slowly open my eyes and breathe deep, trying to control my heartbeat. I stare into the deep blue eyes that are searching my face for any hint of what's about to come out of my mouth.

"I'm completely yours." I press my lips against his and channel all the passion raging throughout my body into one epic kiss.

I rush outside at the sound of the doorbell and snatch the small cardboard box from the porch. A gust of frigid air blows through the kitchen. I step back inside and push the door shut, tossing the box on the table.

"Is Publishers Clearing House outside about to offer us 10 grand?" Lexie trudges into the kitchen rubbing her eyes. "Nothing else is worth getting up this early on a Saturday." She lets out a yawn.

"Dean's Valentine's Day present came." I bounce on my toes and grab the scissors from the junk drawer.

Lexie moseys over to the coffee machine and starts a fresh pot. "Nothing but a stupid commercial holiday."

I shrug. "Yeah, but it's about time I celebrate it." The last time I actually had a date on Valentine's Day was sophomore year with Bobby Johnson. Guess he didn't set the bar too high since he puked all over my shoes after we slugged the awful wine he brought to our Valentine dance. Doubt any date could be that bad. I hop into the wooden chair and nudge the scissors along the packing tape.

Ah, it's in perfect condition. I pull out the baseball from the box and examine the blue letters scribbled in between the red threads. He'll freak when he opens it. This night is going to be epic.

Lexie pours herself a cup of coffee and joins me at the table. "Want a cup?"

I shake my head. "I'm jumpy enough. No caffeine needed."

She glances over the baseball as I hold it up to the

light. "He might propose when he sees that gift." She sips her coffee.

I raise my eyebrows, shrug and stretch a smile across my face. "Who knows, anything can happen."

A small smile graces her face. She sets her cup down on the table. "I'm really psyched for you. He's a great guy."

I nod. "Is this the 'I told you so speech'?"

She sips her coffee and shakes her head. "No way. Who the hell am I to be giving relationship advice? Look at the losers I pick."

I set the baseball back in its box and shove it to the side of the table. "Not everyone is an asshole like Tom."

She slugs down the rest of her coffee. "Yeah, and not everyone is Prince Charming either." She pushes her chair back sending screeches against the tiles and sets her cup in the sink. "A happy medium would do the trick."

"Half-asshole, half Prince Charming. I'm pretty sure that's Jekyll and Hyde." I head over to the fridge and grab a bottle of water.

She shrugs. "He is a doctor."

We burst into a mess of giggles. Leave it to her to find a bright side, even when she's had it with the world of dating. Now, if I could just steal some of her optimism, maybe I wouldn't be a ball of nerves. Sure everything is great...more than great actually, but that could change at any minute, and I'm not sure if I can handle another crushing blow if this turns into a destructive disaster. All I can do is hope Cupid puts some extra magic into that arrow pointed at Dean and I.

I have Dean's gift tucked into my pocket like it's my lifeline on the short walk to the Beta Omega house. It's not like it's even humanly possible to lose it at this point. I run my fingers along the plastic case and take a deep breath, letting the cool air calm my jittery nerves. Everything's different, like the world changed within a week. I look up at the clear blue sky tinged with hints of pink and purple caused by the setting sun. The blistery wave of artic air plaguing us for the last month has turned into a cool forty degree day. Best thing of all, I'm celebrating Valentine's Day with Dean. My stomach flutters like the wings of a million butterflies. Not many guys would risk 'the bond of the Brotherhood' by refusing to take part in one of their biggest parties of the year, Cupid's Bullseye Bash. Then again, Dean Parker isn't most guys.

I turn the corner and trek up the sidewalk to the infamous Beta Omega house. My eyes peruse the drab green siding leading to the wooden inscription above the door. Chills run down my spine spreading goose bumps along my skin. It's like a cloud of dark energy surrounds this place.

I march up the steps and knock on the door. Baseball practice had to start today of all days. Never fails. At least I'll only be spending all of five minutes here tonight while Dean finishes getting ready. Not too bad of a deal. I tap my foot against the black doormat. Seriously? No one can even answer the door.

I sigh. Typical. I loosen my grip on the package tucked tightly in my pocket and slide my hand onto the doorknob, giving it a half-turn. Guess no one worries about locking the door. I step inside and slam the door behind me, making as much noise as possible. God knows what I'm walking into. Anything goes here and I'm not in the mood to walk by any orgies or ritualistic events of any kind.

Great, no reaction. I cautiously walk through the foyer and into the Beta Omega meeting area. More like video game center. Four guys surround the TV, sitting on the couches holding controllers and staring at the screen. No one notices me.

"Hey. Is Dean here?"

"Shit." The TV screen flashes GAME OVER and the guy closest to me drops his controller. He turns toward me. "Hey babe, he's in his room. He'll get to you in a minute." He chuckles under his breath.

It's like I'm in the land of the assholes. How the hell did these idiots even get into college? I huff and spin around. The sooner I get away from them the better. Five minutes has proven to be way too long to spend here. Dean can't take long to get ready. Waiting for him in his room is clearly the lesser of the evils.

I march through the foyer and head up the creaky steps to Dean's room. My pulse races, fluttering faster by the second. Memories of my first encounter here flood my brain. I take a deep breath and slowly exhale, letting all my negative thoughts flow out of my body. Tonight is all about fun and a little romance. I unbutton my black pea coat and pat down my fitted red dress. I'm as ready as I'll ever be. Let the Valentine festivities begin.

I knock and take a step back, hoping Dean likes what he sees. No response. I step forward and knock again. Nothing. I guess knocking on the door is unacceptable behavior in the frat house. I grip the door knob, turning it slowly. I push it open a crack. "Dean?" Nothing. I swing the door open and step inside.

I gasp. My hands fly to my face, covering my mouth. My stomach drops to the floor like a ton of bricks. This can't be happening. I drop my arms to my sides and stare at the scene in front of me, blinking repeatedly. *Please tell me my eyes are playing tricks on me.* Tanya Layton is lying across Dean's bed, half-naked in her red bra and panties, holding a cardboard heart-shaped Valentine. I shift my gaze toward Dean, standing at the head of the bed shirtless wearing only jeans. Bastard.

He holds up his hands and walks toward me. "This isn't what you think."

My hands clench into tight fists. "Please, enlighten me." I look over at Tanya, a smug smile plastered across her face. "You know what? Never mind, I don't want to hear anything you have to say."

A low growl forms in my throat. Maybe she needs someone to slap that smirk from her mouth. My fists clench harder, pressing my fingernails into my palms. I close my eyes tight, trying to suppress the tears that are about to burst from eyes. "Go to hell, both of you."

I turn around and storm out of the room, shoving the door so hard it slams off the wall. A river of tears flows down my cheeks. *God, why didn't I stick to my rules?*

I wipe my cheeks and run down the steps like stampede of horses. I fling open the heavy wooden door like it's made of feathers and fly down the concrete steps. Of course this was destined to go down in a blazing inferno. Just didn't expect it to happen before our first official date.

"Brooke…wait!" Dean yells, trying to pull on his shirt and keep up with me at the same time. He slides it on and runs ahead, stopping right in front of me. We stand face to face in the middle of the road like we're about to have a showdown.

"Leave me alone." I spin around and walk in the other direction. I'd rather walk a million miles out of the way than listen to his bullshit.

He rushes in front of me and stops, blocking my way. "Let me explain." He puts his hands on his knees, trying to catch his breath.

Like any words in the English language are going to change what I just saw. Who's he kidding? He's a frat boy in a frat house who whores around and uses girls just like the rest of those idiots who live there. He almost had me fooled. Dammit! Why did I let myself get involved with him? I wipe a few stray tears from my eyes and lower my head.

He reaches for my arm, but I pull away. "I walked in my room and she was sprawled across my bed. Thought the guys sent her as a joke." He stares with a teary gaze. "Hand to god." He presses his hand against his chest, then raises it in the air.

"Yeah, right. Funny joke." I huff. "You're smarter than that. Can't you think of something better?" I clench my jaw and shoot him a death glare. "Just go. We're done." I take a few steps forward but he refuses to budge.

I turn around again and sprint forward. He catches up to me like I'm not even moving and blocks my path again. "I swear, nothing happened."

"Yet." I push him hard, moving him just enough, and walk forward. I've got to get away. He doesn't deserve the satisfaction of seeing my breakdown.

He steps in front of me again. "Please, stop. You're the only one I want."

"Bullshit!" That's it. I've had enough. Enough of the promises, enough of the lies, and enough of this stupid friggin' holiday. My pulse pounds in my ears like a jackhammer. Adrenaline rushes through my body like a volcano ready to explode. I take a few steps back, stop, and lock eyes with Dean, summing the fires of a thousand hells with one sinister gaze. "Guess what? We can't always get what we want." I stick my hand in my pocket and clutch the baseball. "I don't want a cheater, I don't want a jock, I don't want a frat boy, and I don't want you." I rip the Derek Jeter autographed baseball out of my pocket and launch it with every ounce of energy I have.

The hard ball spins through the air, making contact with Dean's chest. He hunches over from the blunt force. Direct hit to the heart.

CHAPTER 9 — WHITEOUT

I can't take this any more. I push down the silver button on my cell phone until the volume shuts off. Every time that chime sounds through the air it rips open my still-fresh wound. That makes forty-seven texts in less than twenty-four hours. Not one of them answered. One would think he'd take a hint?

I sink into the couch and glance at the cell phone screen out of the corner of my eye.

The recently arrested frat boy won't give up his perfect disappointment without a fight. Please talk to me.

Wow, romance at its finest. Does he seriously think I'll just grab the phone and speed dial his number? No way in hell. Cheating is the ultimate deal breaker. I mean, how am I supposed to trust him after walking in on that scene? Especially since half-naked, drunk girls are just another day at the frat house. Part of me would love to hear what other excuses he devised. Not that anything he says can justify a girl in lingerie laying in his bed.

I just don't get it. He knew I'd be meeting him. Did he think he'd have a quickie then come downstairs to greet me? I grind my teeth. It doesn't add up. He's either a complete idiot or…hmm, I've got nothing.

Lexie stomps through the kitchen like a heard of horses. I flip the heavy fleece blanket to the side and rise from my self-made cocoon of comfort. Guess I can't sulk all day. I march into the kitchen and grab a bottle of water from the fridge.

Lexie slides off her snow-covered boots, setting them on the throw carpet near the door. "It's like a blizzard out there." She shakes the snowflakes out of her hair. "Good news, all classes are cancelled. No physics test for you."

I plop into a kitchen chair and sip my water. "If I had infinity to study for it I'd probably still fail."

She tosses her jacket on the coat rack. "I know a great tutor." She winks.

I huff. "What happened to girl code? Aren't you supposed to hate him too?"

She slides into the kitchen chair and twists her finger around her hair. "Listen. I talked to Olivia and, according to Trevor, Dean is a complete wreck."

I smirk. "Good."

"Anyway. Word is Tanya showed up to the party early,

thinking she was going to score with Dean. I think he was telling the truth. Why not just hear him out?"

I squeeze my bottle of water, crinkling the plastic. A few drops spill over the lid and onto my hand. "What a bitch." Heat flows across my cheeks, creeping up to my ears. "She saw us together at the handcuff party and still pulled her bullshit. What a slut."

Lexie nods and pulls the water bottle from my hand. "According to Trevor, Dean went back to his room after showering and there was Tanya, sprawled on his bed like a hooker." She sets the water bottle on the table. "That's when you showed up."

So, he didn't cheat. A small smile creeps across my face. Alright, guess he's not a complete and total jerk. Maybe I should talk to him, just not yet. I cover my face with my hands rubbing them down to my chin.

Lexie pushes my water bottle toward me and tips her chin. "Tanya was so pissed when Dean ran out on her to chase after you. She was throwing a tantrum like a spoiled brat in front of all the guys." She laughs. "Classic fail."

I let out a small chuckle. "It's about time someone put her in her place. I was kinda hoping it would be me."

Lexie raises an eyebrow. "Go for it."

I shake my head. "It's not worth it. Not now. This crap

probably happens all the time at the frat house."

She leans back in her chair. "Doubt it. Most guys don't leave half-naked girls ready to score in their bed." She rubs her chin. "I'm pretty sure that's never happened, until now.

She's got a point. I nibble at my fingernail. Putting up with all the downfalls of the frat house might kill me. If only he didn't live there, everything would be…perfect. My god, for the first time ever in my nineteen years on this Earth, I found no fault in a guy other than his place of residence. Of course, that happens to be a major fault. Why can't everything just work out for once? Guess perfect doesn't exist.

I sigh. "And I thought sororities were the ones with the drama."

She slides out of her chair and grabs a bag of chips from the cupboard. "Come on, let's find a chick flick with some real drama."

I follow her into the TV room and crash onto the couch, covering myself with my nest of blankets. At this point, the TV dramas have some competition with Beta Omega. I grab the remote and flip through the channels. Awesome, *10 Things I Hate About You.* Kat Stratford had a point. Dating sucks.

Lexie's phone buzzes, scooting across the coffee table.

She picks it up and slightly flinches her head back.

"What?"

She tilts the screen toward me. "It's Dean." She sets the phone between us. "I'm putting him on speaker phone." She presses a few buttons. "Hello."

"Got a second?" His voice shakes.

I lean forward, staring at the phone as if it's the solution to any answers I may seek.

"Yeah, sure," Lexie says.

"Brooke won't talk to me. I need help."

Of course Lexie is 'Team Dean' so she'll help him. I mean, he did take the fall for her with that whole campus police ordeal. Let's just hope she's got 'Team Brooke's' best interests at heart.

"Can you blame her?" Lexie twists hair around her finger.

"Nothing happened. Hand to god." He takes a deep breath and slowly exhales. "She needs to know the truth. I just…I can't stand being without her."

Goose bumps spread across my skin. My heart beats like a drum. The feeling's mutual; being without Dean sucks. No matter what I do, I just can't get him off my mind. So how long am I willing to torture us both?

Lexie covers her mouth with her hand and flashes

puppy dog eyes at me. She drops her hand and clears her throat. "So make her listen, but you'll need some grand gesture to get out of this one."

"Hmm, a grand gesture." His voice lightens. "I'm already devising a plan. Thanks."

"Later." She presses the button to end the call and sets the phone on the coffee table.

I nibble at my fingernails. "I know. I'm going to talk to him."

"What are you so afraid of anyway? He's crazy about you, crazy enough to pour his heart out to your best friend. That says something." She looks over at me still sporting the puppy dog eyes.

I lean back into the couch cushion and stare at the TV. It's at the scene where Kat's at the prom. "Makes me want to run up to him and jump in his arms."

"So what's stopping you?" She pops a few chips in her mouth.

"Don't you remember the last few days? I've got to think rational." I nibble on a chip.

"You think too much."

Doesn't change what the future may hold. "Yeah, but things like this could happen all the time."

"Or they could never happen again."

Yeah, a lot of what-if's in this scenario. Plus what I want and what I need aren't always the same. I just need to clear my head for a minute. "Enough of the Dean and Brooke talk. Let's stare at Heath Ledger for a while."

She raises her eyebrows. "Great idea."

The TV suddenly shuts off, along with all the lights. Dammit. "Guess that idea's shot to hell." *Please, no more relationship talk.*

"I've got an idea. Be right back." Lexie trots down the hallway.

I head over to the window and gaze at the snow-covered road. There's got to be close to a foot out there. Snowflakes dance through the air forming a perfect untouched blanket. It's like a scene from a *Norman Rockwell* painting. Except that not a soul is out on this blustery day.

Lexie walks back to the couch holding a board game. She clears off the table and sets the box down. "Monopoly time."

I chuckle. Monopoly has been our go-to activity whenever there's nothing else to do. Ever since the first night in our apartment when we had an issue with the electric bill. That's when candlelight Monopoly was created. We've also come up with drunken Monopoly, hung-over Monopoly, and I-can't-get-out-of-bed Monopoly.

I scoot down on the floor and grab the thimble, setting it down on the Go space. "Ready to get your ass kicked?" I smirk and grab the dice.

"Bring it on."

Miracles really do happen. I focus on the dice lying on the game board. Yep, eleven spaces. Looks like Lexie's checking into my hotel on Boardwalk. She sighs and moves the silver iron to the blue space.

I hold out my hand. "Someone owes me two grand."

"How about my firstborn?" She tosses her colorful pile of money on the game board. "I'm out."

"Yes!" I yell, throwing my hands in the air in the shape of a V.

"At least you're modest." She grabs the box from under the table and sorts the money into its proper piles.

"Don't you think I'm due for some good luck?" I stand up and stretch my stiff muscles.

She nods and presses the TV remote. "When the hell is

this power going to click back on? We've got two hours of heat if we're lucky."

I shrug. "Guess it's a candlelight dinner for us." I take the game and start toward the hallway.

Music blares, faint at first then slowly getting louder. Is some psycho blasting their car radio and trying to drive in this blizzard? More power to them. I set the Monopoly game on the top shelf and head back into the TV room. A soft melody echoes through the air. Wait, I know this song.

"What's that?" Lexie scrunches her forehead and glances out the window. Her eyes widen. "Um, it's for you." She covers her mouth with both hands.

"What?" I slide the white curtain to the side and search the snow-covered landscape. My heart pounds like a jackhammer. Oh my god, he's insane. Butterflies flutter in my stomach. Dean stands tall, holding up his MP3 player and portable speaker. *In Your Eyes* by Peter Gabriel resonates through the air. I cover my mouth with my hand, an ear-to-ear smile forming underneath, then turn toward Lexie. She flashes those puppy dog eyes yet again. I can't believe he remembered. I drop my hands to my side and desperately try to compose myself. Yeah, like that's going to happen now.

I charge toward the kitchen and fling open the door.

No more rationalizing, no more weighing out pros and cons, no more thinking. Who care's where he lives or what stupid organization he belongs to? He's everything I want.

I step onto the snow-covered porch in my fuzzy blue slippers. Frigid air hits me like a ton of bricks. I shiver even though heat radiates through my veins. Dean trudges through the snow to the first step. A coating of snowflakes decorate his black stocking hat.

He turns down the music and sets a bag on the porch. "Listen. I know you hate me right now but I swear. Nothing happened." He steps up onto the next step. "I won't give up on us. You're worth the fight. I want you. Not Tanya, not any random frat party girls, not anyone else. Only you. I want to make sure that's clear."

I shake my head. "Shut up." I rush toward him and slam my lips to his.

He wraps his arms around me, holding me tight against his red coat.

Lexie claps in the doorway. "That's what I call a grand gesture."

I pull away and take Dean's hand, leading him into the kitchen. He follows, snatching up the bag on the way. We shake the snow from our cold bodies, just dying to feel each other's heat.

Lexie yawns a fake yawn. "See you guys later. Don't be too loud." She winks.

I roll my eyes and chuckle. Once she turns the corner I lunge at Dean. I meet his body lips first and throw all the passion, all the desire inside me into one kiss.

He pulls away, sucking my bottom lip. "I'm not done yet."

I breathe heavily. "Me neither, not even close." I press my lips to his.

He backs up and leans his forehead on mine. "Grand gesture is still in progress." He takes my hand, guiding me into the living room.

I tip my chin and scrunch my eyebrows. "You're full of surprises." I sit on the couch, sinking into the cushion.

He sits next to me, sliding close. "My specialty." He winks. He slides his hand into the wet plastic bag, pulls out a bottle of pink champagne, and sets it on the table. "You know pink's my color."

I giggle, catching my bottom lip in my teeth.

Next, he draws out a pair of novelty handcuffs and swings them around his finger. "Sheriff needs her handcuffs back."

I circle my finger around the cuff and drop them on the couch next to me. "Might have a use for them later." I run my tongue along my lips.

"I like the way you think." He nibbles on his lip then reaches into the bag. "I should've given this to you on Valentine's Day." He sets a blue velvet box on my lap.

I run my fingers along the smooth fabric. My heart races. I've never gotten a gift from a guy before. I flip open the lid. My heart freezes, then pounds. I feather my finger over the delicate silver chain then continue to the shiny silver snowflake pendant engraved with *You're one of a kind*. Tears well in my eyes.

"There can be only one...and that's you."

I leap for him, knocking him back against the cushion until he's lying with me on top of him. "Time for my grand gesture."

He gives me a sweet kiss and reaches his arm down into his bag. "One more surprise." He pulls out a DVD of *Fast Times at Ridgemont High*. Best movie quote ever "When it comes down to making out, whenever possible, put on side one of Led Zeppelin IV'." He grabs his cell phone and presses a button.

Black Dog sounds through the phone's speaker just as the power pops back on.

Like magic, everything comes back to life in one perfect second. I smack my lips against Dean's. His heart thumps through his chest. The heart that now belongs to me. My perfect blissful Valentine.

About the Author

Romance author by night, pharmacist by day, Amy Gale loves rock music and the feel of sand between her toes. She attended Wilkes University where she graduated with a Doctor of Pharmacy degree. In addition to writing, she enjoys baking, scary movies, rock concerts, and reading books at the beach. She lives in the lush forest of Northeastern Pennsylvania with her husband, six cats, and golden retriever.

Visit Amy L. Gale on her Website and sign up for her newsletter

More By Amy L. Gale

Blissful Tragedy:

Ambitious twenty-two-year-old Lexie Waters is intent on taking the advertising world by storm. When she's offered the soon-to-be open position she's been vying for at a swanky advertising agency, there's only one last summer separating her from dreams of corporate success. Still bitter from catching her boyfriend cheating, she heads out for a night of fun to see her favorite band, Devil's Garden, but fun turns into utter embarrassment when she insults the enticingly confident lead singer, Van Sinclair.

Van is intrigued by Lexie's ability to resist his charm and secretly obtains her cell number. Shocked but eager to get to know this captivating rocker, Lexie accepts Van's invitation to see his next show, which requires an overnight stay. The overwhelming feelings that follow take them both by surprise, and with two months left before starting her sought after new position, Lexie joins the tour. As she's catapulted into the world of groupies and wild parties, she questions Van's commitment to her.

So what happens at summer's end when time runs out?